Palma Harcourt was bo
and educated at St Ann
worked in various bran
travelling widely and li
world. Her experiences
background material fo
settings.

CW01663069

Also by Palma Harcourt

THE TWISTED TREE
A TURN OF TRAITORS
TOMORROW'S TREASON
A SLEEP OF SPIES
AGENTS OF INFLUENCE
AT HIGH RISK
A FAIR EXCHANGE
CLIMATE FOR CONSPIRACY
SHADOWS OF DOUBT
THE DISTANT STRANGER

PALMA HARCOURT

Dance for Diplomats

Futura

A Futura Book

Copyright © Palma Harcourt 1976

First published in Great Britain in 1976
by William Collins Sons & Co Ltd

All rights reserved
No part of this publication may be reproduced, stored in a retrieval system, or transmitted, in any form or by any means without the prior permission in writing of the publisher, nor be otherwise circulated in any form of binding or cover other than that in which it is published and without a similar condition including this condition being imposed on the subsequent purchaser.

ISBN 0 7088 2573 7

Reproduced, printed and bound in Great Britain by
Hazell Watson & Viney Limited,
Member of the BPCC Group,
Aylesbury, Bucks

Futura Publications
A Division of
Macdonald & Co (Publishers) Ltd
Maxwell House
74 Worship Street
London EC2A 2EN
A BPCC plc Company

For my goddaughter

This book is fiction. Naturally, some geographical locations and the names of some official and other appointments exist in reality. However, any connection between the characters in this novel and persons who hold or have held these appointments is entirely coincidental.

Chapter 1

I stood at the foot of Guy's grave and tried not to weep. The earth, sodden after the morning's rain, was spreading over the grass. Across one corner the footprints of a dog or some other animal were clearly visible. The vicar had told me that it would be weeks before the gentle mound of earth had settled enough to permit the plot to be turfed and edged with stone. At the moment it looked neglected and bereft, which was precisely how I felt.

Today was my birthday. And not a single person had remembered! I wished I could have forgotten. It was my forty-fifth birthday, and that in itself was no cause for rejoicing. Yet, if Guy had been alive, it wouldn't have mattered. There would have been presents on the breakfast table, some special surprise planned for the day, and tonight we should have been going out to dinner; he had always made a great thing of special occasions. But Guy was dead and I missed him, horribly, which was why I had come up here.

I was saved from an extreme of self-pity by a child's football which, bouncing across the gravel path, suddenly landed with a squelch in the middle of Guy's grave, where it squatted incongruously. It was pursued by its owner, a tousle-headed boy of about seven, who stopped short in his tracks when he saw where his ball had landed. He stared at me, at the ball, and back at me. He took two steps forward and hesitated, waiting for me to bend and retrieve his treasure.

'It wasn't me what did it, miss,' he said in his soft Cotswold burr. 'It was the man what kicked it.'

'Not to worry,' I said. 'Here! Catch!'

I threw the ball towards him and, after some fumbling, he managed to get hold of it. I thought he would run off then but he didn't. Instead, clutching the ball in his arms, he came close up to me.

'The man was watching you, miss,' he said.

'What man?'

'There – by the big angel.'

He turned, pointed in the general direction of the Victorian monstrosity which dominated the churchyard, and fled. A man emerged from the shadow of Gabriel's wing. He was tall, lean, middle-aged and something about the way he walked suggested that he was or had been a soldier. He was also completely self-assured. If he had been watching me – and God knows why he should have been – he was not the least embarrassed at having been caught out. Smiling and unhurried, he advanced on me.

'Lady Rayle?'

'Yes. I'm Catherine Rayle.'

'I called at the house and your housekeeper told me I would find you here. I hope I'm not disturbing you.'

While he spoke he seemed to be inspecting me. Tiny frown-marks appeared between his eyes and as quickly disappeared; obviously he found me wanting – with some justification. I was not, alas, looking my best.

Birthday reaction had caused me to exhume from the back of the wardrobe a trouser suit that had lost its shape and should have been discarded years ago. The blouse and the sandals matched the suit only in decrepitude. And, more self-pity, I had postponed washing my hair until after dinner. The fact that all this was out of character – normally I'm meticulous about my person and I love good clothes – didn't make it any better. I could hardly tell him so. Anyway, it was none of his business!

'My name's Dick Tindle,' he said. 'To be precise, General Sir Richard Tindle. I was a friend of your husband's.'

'Really,' I said. 'I thought I knew most of Guy's close friends.'

'I wasn't a close friend – more a friendly acquaintance, I suppose. And an admirer, of course.'

'I see.'

But I didn't see. Guy had been a good, kind man. He had been a Member of Parliament for years, holding down a safe Conservative seat, and his constituents, to whom he had devoted a great deal of time and energy, had loved him. He had been an able back-bencher, a dependable committee member, liked and respected in the House, but due to some lack either of ambition or ability he had never held high office. It seemed to me a little odd that a mere 'friendly acquaintance' should claim to be an admirer.

'I've been lunching with some people who live not far from here,' he continued bravely, 'and, as I was passing, I thought I would take the opportunity of offering you my condolences – somewhat belatedly, I'm afraid.'

'Thank you,' I said, wondering how he could have been 'passing' when the village was tucked into a fold of the hills and couldn't have been on his way from anywhere to anywhere.

Idly, because it was possible that I might have known them, I asked him who the friends were with whom he had been lunching. He seemed to hesitate. Then he mentioned an unusual name which I couldn't place for the moment though it was familiar enough. I was frowning over it when I noticed him staring at my old sandals again, so I glanced down and, with a mixture of horror and amusement, realized that it wasn't the sandals that fascinated him. It was my feet. Inadvertently, before he had approached me, I had been kicking at the soil of Guy's grave and my feet were filthy.

I started to walk along the path that led out of the churchyard, leaving him to follow if he wished. In two or three strides he caught up with me. I took him the way I had come, not by the village but across a field where Guy's mare and her foal were grazing, through the wood and the kitchen garden to the front of the house. There, as I had hoped, his car was parked. I had to ask him in, but merely as a gesture; considering how ungracious I had been – and my dirty feet – it never occurred to me that he would accept the invitation.

'I'm afraid it's rather late for tea,' I said, 'but, if you haven't too long a drive ahead of you, perhaps you would care to come in for a drink.'

'How charming of you, Lady Rayle,' he said. 'I should love to.'

Months later he told me that my expression at this point was such that it was all he could do not to laugh in my face. On the other hand, when I stuck out my chin and swept into the house ahead of him, he decided that he might not have been wasting his time on me after all. At any rate he followed me meekly. I led him into the drawing-room, showed him where the drinks were and excused myself.

'I must go and change,' I said. 'I'm expecting some friends a little later. I shan't be long.'

I was fifteen minutes. Five minutes under the shower, from head to toe inclusive. Five minutes to blow-dry my hair. Five minutes to dress. I felt better. I took an extra thirty seconds to look at myself in the glass and was as satisfied as I ever am.

I'm five feet ten inches tall. I have narrow feet, long legs, a small bottom, good breasts – and there my luck runs out. I was born with a dowager's hump; no amount of remedial exercises or wearing of painful braces as a child ever made any difference to it. I would have settled for being merely round-shouldered but my little hump thrusts forward my neck and, since I have fawn-coloured hair and large amber eyes, my natural resemblance to a camel is such that even the dimmest of my students – I'm a history don at Oxford – never has trouble finding a nickname for me.

I went downstairs.

My unwelcome guest got to his feet. I hadn't overdone it. I had on a heavy silk blouse, a straight skirt and the handmade kid pumps which I always wear in the house. For a moment he looked at me, his mouth twitched and he gave a little nod of approval. I was both annoyed and pleased. It was an absurd situation.

He had helped himself to a whisky and soda but the drink was barely touched. Reluctantly I poured myself some sherry and sat down. I wondered what we were going to talk about. We had exhausted the subject of Guy on the way from the churchyard; as Tindle had admitted, they had not been close friends. Indeed I couldn't imagine why he had bothered to call;

a letter would have been more than adequate. But he was here and we had to make some conversation.

'Do you live in London?' I asked.

'Yes. I have a flat overlooking Regent's Park but I travel a lot. I've been in Austria for the last few months, which is why I didn't hear at the time of your husband's death or I would have written. Do you know the country?'

'Only from ski-ing holidays and I've been to Vienna a couple of times.'

'Ah – yes. Vienna's one of my favourite cities. There's nothing like the *Torte* at Sacher's or the *Einspanner* in the cafés, is there?'

'Our main reason for going was the opera. Guy was a great opera-lover.'

'But you prefer ballet.' It was a flat statement.

'Yes, I do. How – how did you know?'

'An assumption from what you said about your husband being an opera buff. I share your preference for ballet myself. Anna de Lisle is an old friend of mine. Have you ever seen her dance?'

'Yes, when I was a girl. She was wonderful.'

For a while we talked about ballet. He was far more knowledgeable than I was, and some of his stories, especially about Anna de Lisle, were fascinating. Without thinking, I offered him another drink. His protest was half-hearted.

'You said you were expecting some friends. I don't want to intrude, Lady Rayle.'

I had forgotten my lie, my excuse for changing out of my dirty old clothes. 'There was nothing definite,' I said hurriedly. 'They mayn't come.'

He poured himself another whisky and me some more sherry and began to talk about Austria again. He read me a short lecture on the political situation, or what he thought was the political situation, in that country. For some reason he was convinced that because there was something of a swing to the right, there was going to be a strong left-wing backlash and that, as a consequence, Austria – a dull and peaceful place since the four occupying powers had bowed out in the mid 'fifties and left her as a working democracy – was about to become the vortex of communist activity in Europe. He seemed to feel strongly about it and, as a theory, it was quite intriguing, but I couldn't rouse much enthusiasm for it, not today at any rate. I wished I hadn't pressed him to stay.

'But who am I to be preaching to you, Lady Rayle?' he said, surprising me. 'Modern Europe's your special field, isn't it?'

'Yes,' I said, 'it is.' And unable to resist the dig, I added: 'You're very well informed about the Rayles, Sir Richard.'

He didn't answer and I glanced at my watch. This time he was prepared to take a hint. Five minutes later, after many thanks and renewed expressions of admiration for Guy and regret at his death, General Sir Richard Tindle eased his Bentley away from my front door and disappeared down the drive. He left me with a feeling of vague disquiet, but at least I had got over my maudlin self-pity. I was grateful to him for that.

The next morning I drove into Oxford, garaged the car as usual and walked to the College. I hadn't got beyond the porter's lodge when I was met by one of my colleagues bursting with news. The Senior Tutor had collapsed in chapel and had been whisked off to the Radcliffe Infirmary with peritonitis. I was sorry about the Senior Tutor, who was a very nice man, but I found myself landed with his third-year students which made a lot of extra work and I wished his appendix had refrained from blowing up until the vacation. As it was, the last two weeks of the Hilary Term were to be desperately busy and full of frustrations and petty irritants. But I wasn't allowed to forget Dick Tindle completely.

My first reminder of him was unpleasant and coloured the second. One of my brighter but lazier students was trying to sell me the story that his essay on the history of the North Atlantic Treaty Organization, which he should have brought to the tutorial, had been left at the Lame Duck, where he had spent the previous evening. The Lame Duck is a pub about equidistant from the City of Oxford and my house in the Cotswolds. Guy and I had been there at least half a dozen times; it is an excellent place for dinner – or Sunday luncheon. And now I remembered where I had heard the name of the people with whom Dick Tindle had said he had lunched last Sunday. Indeed he might well have done, because the name belonged to the landlord of the Lame Duck. This meant that Tindle had lied to me, or as near as damn it. He had certainly led me to suppose that he had driven down from London to visit personal friends and, happening to be in the neighbourhood, had decided almost on impulse to call on me. In actual fact, the call would seem to have been the sole object of his expedition and that made no sense, no sense at all.

'Lady Rayle?'

'Ye – es.'

'Is something the matter? You can't really be as angry as you look, not just about an old essay. Or can you?' The boy gave me an appealing smile, such as would make a nonsense in the future of the poor degree that he would doubtless get. 'If you are, I shall buy you off – with a secret.'

'What secret?'

If he wanted to waste the hour I didn't much care; the girl who should have been sharing the tutorial with him had telephoned to say she was unwell. And my mind was only half on what he was saying. With his next words, however, he seized all my attention; Dick Tindle was forgotten.

'Lady Rayle, did you know that the Special Branch was checking up on you?'

'What?'

I was in no mood for jokes and told him so, but he swore it was the truth. 'On my honour, Lady Rayle, I'm not having you on. I was filling in at a dinner-party because the numbers had gone wrong and my mother had a woman too many. Otherwise she wouldn't have asked me. It was a high-powered affair.' He laughed at the memory of it; his father was something important in the City and his mother fancied herself as a political hostess. 'Anyway, when I said I was reading history at Oxford and you were my tutor I saw this chap's ears prick, and after dinner he cornered me and asked me all sorts of questions about you. Cross my heart and hope to die, Lady Rayle. I'm not fibbing.'

'What sort of questions?'

'All sorts – like the liquorice. What your students thought of you and how you spent your money and how many lovers you had – '

'What?'

'Well – er, not in so many words.' He grinned at me.

'Who was this man?'

He told me the name, which meant nothing to me, and reiterated that his father had said he was 'high up in the Special Branch or something like that'. Improbable as the story sounded, I couldn't doubt that it was basically true. And I was the more inclined to believe it because at lunch-time that day I had met my bank manager in the Turl, and he had mentioned that one of the more esoteric private banks had been enquiring about my worth. Altogether it was a little unnerving.

The Bursar was unlucky to choose this particular moment to ask when I would be vacating my rooms. I told him that I hadn't the remotest intention of moving out of College.

'But, Catherine, you know what a shortage of rooms there is in College and, if you're to take up a Government post, surely – '

'What post?' I demanded.

'I – I really don't know. The Master said . . .'

So I sought the Master and, eventually, tracked him down in the Senior Common Room where he was taking sherry before dining in Hall. He was his usual suave self – he had been elected Master on his fund-raising ability rather than his scholarship – and he assured me that he had it on the highest authority that I would soon be asking for a sabbatical in order to pursue more worldly aims. In which case, owing to the lack of College accommodation, I could scarcely blame the Bursar if . . . Since he refused to name his source or the worldly aims that I was expected to pursue and dismissed my avowal of ignorance with an airy wave, the conversation got me nowhere.

Feeling bloody-minded I returned to my rooms where the telephone was ringing shrilly. The receiver, when I picked it up, made a rude noise in my ear. Then a voice I didn't recognize said: 'Lady Rayle?'

'Yes.'

'Good evening. Dick Tindle here. How are you?'

'Very well, thank you,' I said coldly; he hadn't picked his time well either.

'And busy, I imagine, with the end of term?'

'Yes.'

'Then I won't keep you. I telephoned to ask if you would dine with me one night next week. It would be a great pleasure.'

'Where do you suggest? The Lame Duck?'

There was a pause and he laughed. 'That was very stupid of me, wasn't it? But I can explain. Would Wednesday suit you?'

'No, I'm afraid not. I'm – going abroad,' I lied.

'When?' he demanded. 'I must see you before you go.'

'That won't be possible. Goodbye, Sir Richard. Thank you for your invitation.'

'Lady Rayle.'

'Yes.'

'Please reconsider. It really is very important that we should meet. I don't want to go into it on the telephone, but – '

'Goodbye, Sir Richard.'

I put the receiver down firmly and stood looking at it, daring it to ring again. When it remained silent I poured myself a strong whisky, added a little soda and sat in the window-seat staring across the lawns to the line of willows that marked the course of the Isis. Why, I asked myself, had I suddenly become such an object of curiosity to so many people? My past, if not impeccable, contained no skeletons, my present was unexceptional and my future likely to be downright dull.

Two or three weeks later I went up to London to spend a few days with some very old friends of mine. The invitation had been unexpected as they had only just returned from a posting in Belgrade, but more than welcome. I had already begun to ask myself what I was going to do with my vacation; the concept of a pleasant, idle time was beginning to have overtones of restlessness and loneliness. I don't know what was the matter with me; I suppose it was missing Guy.

My first night the only other guest at dinner, obviously by prearrangement, was Dick Tindle.

My host introduced him as 'a colleague from the Foreign Office whom I'm sure you remember', and after the meal we were left alone together, with the coffee. It was all done with an effortless ease that I found both admirable and absurd. Dick Tindle stood by the window – the curtains had not yet been drawn – and stared across the river to the lights on the South Bank. He began to explain himself.

'Lady Rayle – ' he sounded rather sad – 'I often use people. It's part of my job. I want to use you – if you're willing. But perhaps I had better make it clear that, although it's true I'm in the Foreign Office, I'm not a diplomat. I am, in fact, in Intelligence.'

'And – and you want to use me? Whatever for? As a spy?'

'Oh God – no!' he said, and added unflatteringly: 'How I wish the stupid public would get it out of their heads that Intelligence is synonymous with espionage. Only a fraction of Intelligence is cloak-and-dagger stuff. And I am *not* asking you to sell your honour on some Mata Hari couch, Lady Rayle. What I – '

'That's lucky,' I said calmly. 'I don't think I'd be much good at that sort of thing.'

He had the grace to laugh. 'Sorry,' he said. 'Look, give me some more coffee – I can't bear these thimblefuls – and let me tell you about it.' He came and sat opposite me. 'You recall what we were talking about at dinner, the weakness and apathy of NATO? Well, it's far worse than anyone believes. By next spring the Americans intend to have withdrawn all their troops from Europe; they've threatened this before but now they're really going to do it. They're fed up with allies who won't co-operate and who bicker amongst themselves. For their part the Europeans are fed up with being treated as satellites. So, unless something is done about it, NATO will disintegrate and the countries of Western Europe, who unfortunately seem incapable of co-operation with each other, will lie open to Russian influence. My present job is to ensure that something *is* done about it and that we're not picked off one at a time. And I need your help.'

He paused to sip his coffee and I said: 'My help? I admit you have my sympathy but I can't imagine how I can help.'

'I can,' he said gently. 'You see, by now I know a great deal about you.'

'Yes,' I said, thinking how slow I had been on the uptake. 'You must do. It's you who has been asking all those questions about me, starting rumours and – '

'Please! I'll confess everything. First, I wasn't a friend of your late husband's. I never met him. That was an excuse to meet you on your home ground, to look you over. As for the questions and rumours, as you say, I'm responsible for those too. I had you vetted by the Security Service. I had to be certain that you were suitable and available.' He smiled at me.

'For God's sake, what for?' I didn't feel like returning his smile.

'To be our next Permanent Representative to NATO – our permanent member of the North Atlantic Council in Brussels.'

'What? You must be joking.'

'I've never been more serious.'

'In that case you're mad, stark, staring mad!'

'I've been told that before, but madness sometimes pays high dividends. I'm hoping it will in this case.'

'But why me?'

'We need somebody to replace the present ambassador who is going on to bigger and better things this summer, somebody who knows Europe and what makes Europe tick, somebody who feels strongly that the Western Alliance is the best defence, perhaps the only defence, against the spread of communism and – ' he paused – 'somebody who is prepared to shout it from the rooftops. You see, the choice has narrowed considerably. That somebody has to be a political appointee. A professional diplomat just wouldn't be credible as a crusader – and there are good reasons why it's a crusader we want right now – because no professional diplomat could afford to get so deeply involved. It wouldn't be fair to ask a first-class career man to stake his future in these unusual circumstances. And a lesser man couldn't do it. Do you think you could?'

'I could try, but I don't understand why – '

'Lady Rayle, widow of Sir Guy Rayle, DSO, MP – we would

have to build up your late husband in the public eye a little before your appointment was announced – would be a credible political appointee. Your Oxford background, your expertise, mean that as a person you would be taken seriously. And there's some spin-off. You already have a handle to your name so there's no need to create a new knight or, God forbid, a dame to match the appointment, and you speak fluent French – the other NATO language. What more could one ask?'

'To resurrect Jeanne d'Arc perhaps.'

He laughed. 'I'm sure that won't be necessary. You have the cause in which you believe, the voices will come from the Foreign Office, and – '

Deliberately he looked me up and down as he had done the first time we met, by Guy's grave. Now, however, sitting in a high-backed chair, in a long velvet skirt and my Hermes blouse, I was conscious of looking my best. And, oddly enough, this time I didn't resent his impudence. My chin came up and I waited for the verdict.

He said: 'Although she consorted with kings and was said to have been beautiful, Jeanne d'Arc was only a peasant girl. Somehow I don't think she'd have been my choice for this job. You are, Lady Rayle.'

'Thank you,' I said, mocking the compliment even though it pleased me. 'But may I remind you that Jeanne d'Arc had an army behind her. I don't understand what you expect me to achieve by myself. However hard I worked at it and however hard I beat the drums, I couldn't really hope to be the saviour of Europe.'

'No, of course not,' he said, 'but you could help. This job, which you'll be offered formally, of course, is important, even essential, though I admit that it's only the tip of the iceberg. The rest – well, you'll have to leave that to other people. We'll try not to let you down.' He grinned at me. 'You will do it, won't you? You'll head the UK Mission to NATO when the present chap goes?'

If the offer had been made while Guy was alive there would have been no question whatsoever of accepting it, but now . . . A year, two years in Europe – away from the frustrations of the university and the present heartaches of my home in the Cotswolds – why not?

I drew a deep breath and expelled it slowly. 'Yes,' I said. 'I'll do it.'

Thus, with scarcely more than a single dither, I, Catherine Rayle, agreed to become the United Kingdom Permanent Representative to the North Atlantic Council.

Chapter 2

We were descending through cloud-layers and the plane was bumping; the Fasten Safety Belts notice had lit up. My glass slithered towards me. I caught it and finished what champagne was left. Almost immediately the steward was beside me, bracing himself against my empty aisle seat. This was an afternoon flight on the first Sunday in September and we were carrying a full load, but HMG had seen fit to provide me with two seats. I was sitting in the one by the window; the other had come in useful for the Sunday newspapers and for my bag containing the red diplomatic passport issued by the FCO only to ambassadors.

'A little more champagne, Lady Rayle?'

'Thank you.'

I should have said no, but my throat was dry, even though I had been drinking champagne since take-off and Dick Tindle had insisted on wine with lunch before we drove to the airport; it had been good of him to see me off in such style. The Minister and other members of the Mission would be meeting me at Brussels National. I sipped the champagne. I told myself it was the smoked salmon I had eaten that was making me feel so parched, though more likely it was nerves. I thought of asking for a glass of water but the pilot had already put down his wheels. I finished the champagne as the No Smoking sign went on and the steward was beside me again.

'Thank you, no,' I said firmly.

'But, Lady Rayle! Your hands!' He was leaning over me, hissing in my ear. 'It's the ink, my – dirty!' He had almost forgotten himself and called me 'my dear', but he recovered quickly. 'You've been reading the papers, Lady Rayle, and the newsprint – I sometimes think the Sundays are worse than the dailies.'

I took the small, hot towel which he was holding out to me in a pair of plastic tongs and cleaned my hands on it. They were black with printers' ink – not at all *à la mode* for an ambassador! I gave the damp towel back to him and accepted a dry one; my hands now smelt of eau-de-Cologne, which was very pleasant. And by the time this pantomime was over and he had bustled away with towels, newspapers and champagne glass, we were out of the cloud-cover. The sun was shining. Belgium, neat and tidy, lay below me.

The plane banked and began its final descent. Canned music blared over the intercom. My ears hurt. I swallowed and swallowed again. We touched down, the engines screamed with the reverse thrust and the safety-belt bit into my middle. The pilot had made a perfect landing and this, I hoped, was a good omen. Anyway it was too late now to have cold feet.

We taxied around the runways, bumping gently over the joins in the concrete and came to a stop somewhere in the out-field. There was an irritable murmur from some of my fellow-passengers, who resented the indignity of having to be embussed instead of arriving at a bay. This was stilled as the steward hurried from seat to seat in the first-class compartment, bent low, muttered into ears; he didn't come to me and I thought I caught the words 'ambassador' and 'Lady Rayle'. The couple across the aisle were staring and I looked through them. The stewardess brought my coat, a fine mink – the last present that Guy had given me – and I draped it over my arm; it was too warm to wear it. I sat, like everyone else, waiting. I felt very nervous.

It seemed a long wait, but, eventually, the steps were adjusted, the doors were open and the steward escorted me from the plane. For a moment I stood on the platform and looked down. The place was littered with machinery and people. There were the usual baggage men in dirty white overalls, manœuvring bright yellow vehicles, two buses to transport the passengers, a Rolls-Royce with a uniformed chauffeur beside it and, at the bottom of the steps, my reception committee standing together in a bored fashion.

I started down, and a lot of things happened at once.

The day was beautiful and sunny, the temperature 16 degrees Centigrade, but there was a gusty wind. Suddenly it flipped the fur coat I was carrying around my legs. The steps shuddered in the blast. A flash of sun, reflected off glass or metal, shone in my eyes, blinding me. I stumbled, felt my hand slip on the rail and pitched forward. As I fell there appeared among the three upturned faces floating below me the face of Hugo Pewter whom I hadn't seen for almost twenty years.

They caught me. To the startled steward and stewardess in the doorway behind me it must have looked like a circus act, even if the star was rather out of practice. I flew through the air with no great ease, encumbered by my damned coat and the need to retain hold of my bag, and as the tarmac rushed to hit me I was uplifted by three pairs of strong arms and set on my feet. There I stood, swaying slightly and fighting to get my breath, while the three men smiled smugly at me. And Hugo, Hugo supported me gently by one elbow.

'Lady Rayle – Catherine,' he said, 'how very, very nice to see you again.'

Holding me as he was by one arm, I suppose that he couldn't have offered to shake my hand but surely there was no need for him to kiss me, a peck on each cheek. And to call me Catherine! He had never called me Catherine in his life; it had always been 'Kit' or some endearment. Damn his eyes!

I let him lead me away from the steps – the other first-class passengers were now threatening to descend – in the direction of the Rolls. We grouped ourselves by the car.

Hugo said: 'May I present David Driscole, Head of Chancery.'

'Lady Rayle.'

David Driscole bowed over my hand. He was a short, dark man with a large nose and a clever, ugly face. He apologized for the fact that his wife was not with him.

'She hopes you'll excuse her, Lady Rayle, but it's the last weekend before the children go back to school and – and she hasn't been very well lately.'

'Daphne sends her apologies too,' Hugo said, assuming I would remember the name of the woman whom he had married, 'but such a lovely Sunday afternoon . . .' He left the sentence to explain itself and turned to the youngest member of the party. 'And this is Simon Maryton, who's to be your Private Secretary.'

'How do you do, ma'am,' Simon Maryton said, as if he were addressing royalty. He bowed and came forward to shake hands. 'Fortunately I don't have a wife to incommode.'

I gave him a thin smile. His remark had been unnecessary. I had already appreciated the point. I had shown my ignorance of the diplomatic way of life by choosing to arrive on a Sunday; I had spoiled the weekend without excuse. I should have realized or Dick Tindle should have warned me. Nevertheless, I resented the unstated reproof. Abruptly I turned away from them, greeted Rule, the chauffeur, whom I had previously met in London, and let him help me into the car.

Passport and Customs clearance had been arranged beforehand and my baggage was collected with maximum speed. In no time Brussels National was receding behind us. I forced myself to relax in the comfort of the Rolls – and not to avoid touching Hugo, who was sitting beside me, as we wound around corners. Fortunately I had little to do but listen. The conversation was casual. It was mainly about the Residence, convenient for NATO and the airport, close to the Forêt de Soignes if one liked to ride or walk, and with easy access to downtown Brussels. They sang its praises so blithely that I began to wonder what the snags were.

When I saw the place I no longer cared if there were a hundred snags. If I couldn't have one of those tall, thin houses with a laddered roof in the heart of the city, which was what I really hankered after, then this was for me. I had been told that the Residence, which HMG had bought very recently, was a hideous house in a snob suburb. What I had not been told was that, although it had no claim to any architectural style or merit, it had enormous character, and was set on the side of a hill in about three acres of garden which included a small maze. At once I decided that I could be happy there.

'Very happy, I hope,' Hugo said and added, gratuitously I thought, 'I gather it was originally built for one of the royal mistresses.'

'Really?' I said. 'How times change.'

I sipped the Perrier with a splash of whisky that I neither needed nor wanted. I had felt compelled to offer the three men a drink, though I had made it very clear that the invitation was optional. David Driscole, seizing his chance, had refused and Rule was driving him home, but until the car returned I was stuck – or so I assumed – with Hugo and young Maryton.

Hugo, however, showed not the slightest desire to linger. Having explained that he would meet me the next morning at NATO Headquarters, introduce me to the UK Delegation and the top brass of the International Staff, both civilian and military, and escort me to luncheon with the Secretary General, he said that he really must go. It seemed that he and his Daphne were neighbours of mine. If I walked up through my garden and along a little lane I could arrive at the back entrance of their house in six or seven minutes; Daphne and the wife of the former ambassador, who had been very good friends, had always been 'popping in' on each other.

There was the faintest hint of malice in this last remark of Hugo's and I wondered what he had told his wife about me – nothing, I hoped, to make her dislike me. I could do without that sort of complication.

He said his goodbyes and strolled off up the hill, taking Simon with him. Simon – and this was another blow – was to live at the Residence. To judge from his scowl he didn't like this any more than I did, but Hugo had decided that the arrangement was necessary and it was impossible to question it, at least for the moment. Simon had already moved into a suite of rooms.

I watched them go with relief. I was glad to be alone. And yet, irrationally, I resented being left by myself on my first night in Brussels and having to eat a cold meal at one end of a dining-room table that could seat twenty. In Daphne's place I would have . . .

But I refused to think of Daphne and Hugo until I was less fraught. I went upstairs, bathed, changed, took some aspirin and did a little unpacking. During supper I read and afterwards, since it was still light and since I still had the remains of a champagne and tension headache, I explored the garden. This was more delightful than I had supposed, but nothing could take my mind off my problem – if indeed it was a problem. I sat on a garden bench and thought about it, as I had done many times since I had been briefed on my staff-to-be.

It was all so bloody silly! I had met Hugo Pewter at the end of my second year at Oxford. Somebody's mother, who knew my parents and who was footing the bill, had decided that I should be included in her son's party to a Commem. Ball. It was typical of the invitations that I received and typical of me that I should have accepted. I was a wooden dancer and expected to hate the whole affair. And so I did, until Hugo woke me from the depths of my refuge in a deckchair by pouring champagne over me. We strolled around the lake together and watched the dawn break, blushing the waters and the sleeping swans, and later, after we had breakfasted by the river, Hugo drove me home. That was the nice, simple, romantic beginning of it.

It could well have been the end of it too. But Hugo, for God knows what reason, decided otherwise. The following term we became lovers and he took me seriously in hand. He taught me about clothes and what to do with my hair and not to mind my little hump but to be proud of myself. He was extraordinarily kind to me. When we went down from Oxford we took a flat together in Chelsea; Hugo was then at the Foreign Office and I was working for a doctorate at London University. It was tacitly accepted among our friends and by my disapproving parents – Hugo's didn't seem to care a damn – that as soon as Hugo was established we should marry. However, since the Office frowned on early marriages and we were perfectly happy as we were, the question did not really arise. Then Hugo was posted as Third Secretary to the Embassy in Prague and within six months had married the ambassador's seventeen-year-old daughter.

For a while I thought it was the end of the world; but I survived. Indeed, I more than survived. A fellowship at my old Oxford college, work that I enjoyed, a very satisfying marriage – I had had enough of high romance – everything had helped. Now, surely, there could be no problem, unless I chose to make one. All I had to do was remember that I was Her Excellency, Lady Rayle and Hugo was Hugo Pewter, CMG, Minister and Deputy Permanent Representative. He was my deputy! Poor old Hugo, who had always been exceedingly ambitious – my deputy. It was an ironic situation but no problem. Too much champagne during the flight, falling down the aircraft steps, actually meeting Hugo after so many years, had made a fool of me. It wouldn't happen again, I told myself. The past was very dead.

Yet I remained conscious of a slight uneasiness, perhaps because I hadn't been altogether frank with Dick Tindle. When I had been told the name of my Minister, I had merely said that I had known him at Oxford. If Dick's ferrets had failed to dig up the dirt about Hugo and me, the fault was theirs, I had argued, and, anyway, it wasn't relevant. I went to bed and tried to sleep.

At two o'clock in the morning I was still awake and somebody, coming down the hill behind the house, was singing at the top of his voice in an untuneful tenor a rich and bawdy song. Simon Maryton had returned to the Residence after an evening spent carousing with the Minister.

Some weeks later I was getting used to my job.

I sat at the desk in my plush office and with very great care drew a stylized compass rose, which is the symbol of the North Atlantic Treaty Organization. I was meant to be preparing a speech. These days I was always preparing speeches, delivering speeches, writing memoranda, dictating telegrams, button-holing people in the corridors, arguing in committees, making a damned nuisance of myself. But, for all the use my piddling efforts were, I could have been sharing Guy's peaceful, Cotswold grave.

Dick Tindle had been right. There was every reason to worry about what would happen in Western Europe when the Americans went home and NATO's forces became less and less credible, either for war-fighting or as a deterrent. The high-paid help, civilian and military, were aware of this. Few if any of them, however, could persuade their political masters, immured in their respective capitals, of the dangers that lay ahead; meanwhile, they bickered amongst themselves. I sometimes thought that what was needed to reunite the Western Alliance and revitalize its efforts was a bloody good scare.

The intercom buzzed. 'Yes,' I said, glad to have my unpleasant thoughts interrupted.

'Lady Rayle.' It was Simon's voice. 'I've just had Mrs Pewter on the phone. She's hoping to give a reception for the Nuclear Planning people who'll be here at the end of the month. She suggests the 26th but you have the evening crossed out.'

'Yes. Some friends from the French Embassy are taking me to the Bolshoi Ballet.'

'Could you look in before – just for a few minutes perhaps?'

'No, Simon. There won't be time. Please apologize to Mrs Pewter for me, will you?'

His sigh came over the intercom as a groan. I grinned to myself. Simon, in spite of his insistence on by-passing me and referring anything he thought important directly to Hugo, had proved more amenable than I had expected. But Daphne, with her crooked Greek profile, small defenceless body and little girl's voice, was a bitch. She had gone out of her way to feed me sugar-coated pills ever since I had arrived. I was tired of being alternately snubbed and patronized. And it didn't help that Hugo had done his best to deflect her barbs. I was damned if I would risk being late for the ballet by going to a party that Daphne was only giving to upstage me.

I turned to my speech and was making notes when the door was rapped and opened simultaneously. Hugo came in carrying a sheaf of papers.

'Good morning, Catherine. I've brought the figures on national defence expenditures per capita that you said you wanted.'

'Thank you. I'm sorry to have bothered you. I asked the Budget people for them.'

'I know. They thought they needed some explaining, but I've straightened them out so that they're on a comparable basis. However – '

'Simon, dear boy.' The voice of one of the International Staff members came loud and clear over the intercom. 'Is the Lady Amateur at home? If she is, would you tell – '

Hugo leaned over the desk and cut off the braying voice. I stood up, thrusting back my chair so that it hit the wall. The Lady Amateur. I could feel the colour staining my neck, my cheeks. I started towards the door.

'No, Kit! No!' Hugo barred my way. 'You never heard that.'

I swore vividly, in an argot I had learned as a child from a French cousin. Hugo smiled at me with surprising tenderness. I choked.

'I didn't understand half your French but I hope it did you good.' He pulled up my chair. 'Here, come and sit down.'

I sat. 'I had no idea, no idea at all, that that was how – how they thought of me.' I was ready to spit.

'My dear Kit, don't take it so personally. Every political appointee is considered a whore. You must know that. And in this extremely male-oriented society you do rather stick out as a – a lady, especially since you insist on being such a – '

'Go on, Hugo,' I said through my teeth.

'Such a bloody zealot!' he said finally. 'You're meant to be the UK Permrep, Kit, but you behave as if you alone realized the constant threat of communism. Look, most of us here would agree that this period of détente with the USSR is phoney and we'll rue the day we let NATO become meaningless. But you're not going to achieve anything by rubbing people's noses in it.'

'You don't think so?'

'I'm positive. The Office should have briefed you better, and warned you of – various difficulties.'

He was right on the second point at least, I thought later. I didn't understand why Dick Tindle hadn't even mentioned the 'various difficulties', including the one which Hugo had ignored. Everybody had hoped and expected that Hugo himself would get my job. Many – not just Daphne, which was natural – resented the fact that he had not. Perhaps it was no wonder that in the circumstances they should call me the 'Lady Amateur'. But it didn't make it any easier to take.

And I had a nasty suspicion that Hugo could be right on the second count too. I could be going about everything in the wrong way and achieving nothing. I envied Jeanne d'Arc the faith she had in her 'voices'; my trust in Dick Tindle's infallibility was beginning to wane.

Despondent, I thought of putting through a call to London, hesitated, and decided against it. I made a few more notes for my speech and glanced at the tabulated figures that Hugo had brought in. It was impossible to concentrate. I picked up *The Times.* A couple of paragraphs, at the bottom of a column on an inside page caught my eye and, ludicrous as it may seem, raised my spirits.

There had been an incident in Vienna. A public meeting organized by the extreme right had been broken up by students. The riot police had been called and several arrests made. The students themselves were now forbidden to demonstrate; there had been too many such incidents. It had been suggested that they were communist-inspired and, in view of the Federal elections next spring, the situation required firm handling.

This sudden flaring of political violence in hitherto peaceful Austria was precisely what Dick Tindle had forecast the first time we met, that Sunday in the Cotswolds. Illogically, the accuracy of his prophecy did a lot to restore my faith in his judgement. There might be no connection between events in Vienna and my present job, but . . .

On an impulse I dialled Dick's number. Sir Richard Tindle, I was informed, was not at present available. He was out of the country. He was expected back later this evening. I said that it wasn't important and there was no message.

I was in bed, not yet asleep but reading, when Dick telephoned. My anger and embarrassment of the morning had faded and he made short work of my doubts.

'My dear Catherine, you're doing splendidly,' he said. 'Absolutely splendidly. I read every one of the reports and telegrams and you're giving us just what we want. Keep it up!'

'If you're sure – ' I said. After all, Hugo knew nothing of the reasons behind my appointment.

'Positive.'

'Well, I'm sorry to have bothered you, Dick. Thank you for phoning so soon on your return. I hope you had a good trip. Were you in Austria again?'

There was a distinct pause before he answered. 'I had to attend some meetings in Bonn,' he said, 'and very dull they were.'

It's often harder to lie on the telephone than face to face and I could have sworn that he was lying. But it was none of my business and I didn't want to pry. And when he spoke again his voice was no longer flat.

'I was going to telephone you anyway. I'm hoping you'll do something for me, a favour.'

'Of course, if I can.'

'I expect you remember me telling you that Anna de Lisle was an old friend of mine. She can't stand the English winters any longer and always goes down to the South of France. This year she's going via Brussels so that she can see the Bolshoi Ballet. She has half a dozen seats, front row of the balcony, for Tuesday, the opening night.'

'Good God!' I said. 'They're worth their weight in gold.'

Dick laughed. 'I know. And they're for you and your guests, if you'll put Anna up for a night or two at the Residence.'

'I should be honoured, Dick. I don't need a bribe.'

'I'm sure you don't. I told Anna you would be delighted. She was a little diffident about it. And, Catherine – '

'Yes?'

'May I suggest a champagne supper after the ballet. It's *Swan Lake*, incidentally.'

'That will be perfect,' I said. 'I shall look forward to it.'

Chapter 3

'If you don't mind,' Anna de Lisle said, 'I should like to look around the Residence.'

'Now?' I didn't try to hide my surprise.

'When you've finished your coffee,' she said politely.

She gave me a bland smile and stood up, leaning on a gold-knobbed, ebony cane, which she needed because of an arthritic hip. It grieved me to see her limp, though even her limp was not ungraceful; well past sixty now, she still had a fierce control over her once beautiful dancer's body. And her face was still that of a *gamine,* small and pointed, with hair cut short and nut-brown eyes. Her smile widened, became mischievous.

'Pretend that I'm thinking of buying the house,' she said. 'I would like to start at the top and work my way down. And, Catherine, please show me everything.'

'All right,' I said, 'if that's what you want.'

I was mystified. I couldn't imagine why on this, the first evening of her visit, Anna de Lisle should be so very interested in the Residence. Yet she had meant it when she said she wanted to be shown everything. She repeated her request when I overlooked a little sewing-room and, reproached, I opened cupboards for her, pointed out which rooms were connected, told her where stairs led. I let her poke and pry. If this was her idea of after-dinner entertainment I didn't mind. I stopped her only when we came to Simon's suite.

'I'm sorry,' I said. 'We can't go in there.'

'Why not?'

'Those are Simon Maryton's rooms. He's my Private Secretary.'

'Does he live here?' She was startled.

'Yes.'

'Dick never mentioned him,' she said, and before I could stop her she had rapped on the door and opened it.

I followed her in because there was nothing else that I could do. Excuses would have to be made for what Simon would consider an intrusion on my part, if not on Anna's. I had never been in his rooms before. But, as luck would have it, excuses weren't needed. Simon was not at home.

I hovered in the doorway while Anna explored. She took her time about it. Her main interest in the rest of the house had been its layout, but now she inspected the books, the records, the pictures, the photographs; she even spent a minute admiring a beautifully carved jade bird.

'A fascinating young man,' she said and disappeared into his bedroom. Moments later she called me. 'Catherine, come!'

'What is it?'

I found her peering into what one would have assumed to be a cupboard but was, in fact, a door giving on to a steep flight of stairs. The stairs were carpeted, the woodwork free of dust and the electric bulb for which Anna discovered the switch had a pleasant shade.

'Where do they lead?' she asked.

'I have no idea,' I said. 'Miss de Lisle – Anna, please let's go. I really don't want to be caught inspecting Mr Maryton's rooms.'

'I must know where they lead,' she said obstinately.

'Very well! Wait here while I go and see.'

Famous ballerina or not, I thought, controlling my irritation, she was mad, quite mad. I walked carefully down the stairs, which were too narrow to need a hand-rail, negotiated the curves, and came to another door with a spring lock. This opened into the conservatory at the back of the house. I assumed that Simon used the staircase at his convenience and saw no reason why he shouldn't.

I returned to find Anna in Simon's sitting-room, examining the papers on his desk. She followed me without protest into the corridor. She was deep in thought and the main rooms on the ground floor, which she had seen before, didn't rouse her. But she was charming to my cook and houseman, who showed her around their quarters, and she appeared fascinated by the conservatory, with its private entrance to Simon's suite, and by the arrangement of the back premises.

'You must explore the grounds in the morning,' I said with a bite of sarcasm. 'They're very attractive.'

'Yes,' she said firmly. 'I must. Where does your chauffeur live?'

'In – in a flat over the garage. His wife helps in the house if I give a large party. There's also a gardener and a gardener's boy, but they don't live here,' I said.

'And I'm a nosy old woman who desperately needs a brandy after all that stomping about.' She laughed and put a hand on my arm. 'My dear, you're just as Dick Tindle described you. Did you know he was a great admirer of yours? He sang your praises to me.'

I made a noncommittal noise and went to pour the brandy. Reflected in a mirror I saw Anna de Lisle wince as her cane slipped and she sat heavily. In the too bright light from a lamp she looked old and vulnerable and in pain. I reproached myself for being so caustic. I took her the brandy, moved the lamp and sat beside her.

'You're very kind,' she said and, in the same breath, added: 'I suppose you're aware that your Private Secretary listens to your phone calls?'

I stared at her. 'Listens to my calls! He could, of course. All the phones in this house are on the same line. I sometimes hear him when I pick up my receiver. It's very inconvenient and I'm trying to get it changed. But – why should he?'

'He's left some notes on his desk. He seems to be keeping an eye on your movements, too.'

'It's part of his job to know where I am and what I'm doing, though I must admit he often seems over-zealous about it. But phone calls are different. If what you say's right, I shall have to do something about it – and quickly.'

'No. Please don't, Catherine, not for a few days.' And seeing my surprise she smiled at me gently. 'I told you I was a nosy old woman. Well, I am, and with reason – a very good reason.

Dick Tindle didn't request your hospitality for me merely so that I could live in comfort and go to the Bolshoi in style, you know. He hoped that I could plead a cause. A cause in which he and I are very, very interested. In fact, the cause pleads itself. You can't refuse, Catherine.'

I lay awake and thought about it.

Baranov was possibly the greatest living male ballet dancer. He was in his prime. He was superb, and the pride of the Bolshoi Ballet Company. For some reason, not clear to me at any rate, he had recently decided that he was Jewish – he had one half-Jewish grandparent – and he wanted to emigrate to Israel. Having some sense, he had not applied for an exit visa; he knew what had happened to other famous artists who had wished to leave Mother Russia. He had decided to defect.

In my ignorance I had always thought defection to be a relatively simple matter for one in Baranov's position. He was permitted to travel abroad; indeed, he was encouraged to do so with the Bolshoi Company. The KGB could not watch him all the time in Western capitals. He was internationally known. He could if he wanted leap into a taxi and say, in effect: 'I am Baranov. Take me to the Israeli Embassy.' But evidently he didn't like this idea. Anna had explained that he didn't want the Israeli Government to bear the primary blame, for fear of retaliation against his fellow Jews in the USSR.

Instead, he had managed to make contact with someone who had made contact with Dick Tindle; he seemed prepared to trust the British. But, according to Anna, he had insisted that he would defect in Brussels, and only in Brussels. The British were to arrange for him to stay in an absolutely safe place until he could be flown to Israel.

'Why me?' I had asked. 'Why not Sir Thomas Bright, the British Ambassador to Belgium, if it has to be a British Ambassador? Wouldn't he be more suitable than the Ambassador to NATO?'

'No,' Anna had said. 'Sir Thomas is a career man. We can't expect him to compromise himself. He would have to play it by the book. But this isn't a – a straightforward defection to the British Government. Baranov's really just passing through our hands. Catherine, Dick himself is bending the rules to get Baranov safely to Israel and, in these special circumstances, he didn't think it too much to ask you to provide a couple of nights' sanctuary. That's all it amounts to. We thought we could count on you for that.'

'Yes,' I had said doubtfully.

'For God's sake, Catherine, Baranov's one of the greatest dancers of the century. How can you refuse?'

I had not refused; it seemed inhuman to refuse. I hadn't actually committed myself either, not yet. In the morning I proposed to get in touch with Dick Tindle on the secure line from the office and make sure that he confirmed Anna's arrangements. I would tell him of my doubts about Simon, too. And, whatever my feelings, I would do what he wanted. I couldn't refuse, but I could wish like hell that I had not been asked.

The arrangement was that Baranov would be delivered Tuesday after the ballet, spend two or three days at the Residence, and be collected. It would be inconvenient for me, even nerve-racking, because his presence must not be suspected by the servants or Simon – but no worse than that.

I pulled the bedclothes more tightly round my neck. I was cold in spite of the central heating. Perhaps it was nervousness. Anna had made everything sound very simple, too simple. Even I could visualize half a dozen scenarios in which things went wrong. It was hard to sleep.

It was Tuesday evening and the Bolshoi had opened in Brussels. The Théâtre Royal de la Monnaie shook with the applause. The audience was on its feet, clapping, stamping, shouting '*bravo!*' and '*bis!*' and '*encore!*'. The stage was littered with flowers. The curtain began to come down and there were angry cries and boos. Half-way down, it stopped and went up again. After a superb performance of *Swan Lake*, the Bolshoi was taking its umpteenth curtain call. Then somebody shouted 'Baranov!' and immediately everyone took up the cry. 'Baranov!' 'Baranov!'

All the applause, all the adulation, all the flowers, were really for this one man.

He stepped forward and the audience went wild. He bowed, waved, and blew kisses to us. He paid homage to his *prima ballerina* and the *corps de ballet* with whom he would never dance again. It must have been an intensely emotional moment for him. And suddenly it was too much. He sprayed the armful of roses he was carrying, over the heads of the orchestra, into the front stalls and, as a near riot to possess one of Baranov's roses began, he walked off the stage.

Anna touched my arm. 'We must go,' she said.

She nodded at me reassuringly. Her eyes were bright with the tears that had raddled her cheeks and I remembered that Odette/Odile had been her most famous role. She must have been on stage again tonight, dancing with Baranov. Now she was back in the audience, her arthritic hip troubling her, but she had painted a smile on her face. She looked frail but determined. I did my best to respond by showing that I was in control of the situation.

I sent Simon ahead to make sure that Rule was waiting with the car and ushered the rest of our party, as quickly as the still-excited crowd of balletomanes would permit, into the main lobby. There was no sign of Simon. I asked David Driscole to go and look for him. Daphne wandered off to speak to friends. Anna, after sitting for so long in one position, was having difficulty in hiding the fact that she was in pain. Where the hell was the Rolls?

Hugo said: 'Catherine, are you all right?'

'Why shouldn't I be?'

'You're rather tense. Even during the ballet you seemed to be sitting on the edge of your seat – metaphorically speaking.'

'My dear man, I was absorbed!' I glanced around the foyer. 'There's David, I think. But where's Daphne? Hugo, do go and collect your wife.'

'Of course,' he said stiffly.

'I'm sorry,' I said to Anna as Hugo disappeared into the throng. 'Obviously I'm not a very good actress.'

She shook her head at me. 'Nobody would have noticed,' she

said, 'nobody but Hugo Pewter. He knows you so well and he's still very fond of you, my dear.'

If Anna de Lisle had wanted to boost my morale, she had done the reverse. Her use of the word 'still' had been a clear give-away. She could know nothing of me except what she had learned from Dick Tindle, which meant that Dick must have known all along about Hugo and me. Yet he had never so much as hinted . . .

I heaved a sigh. This was not the moment for worrying about personal relationships. I needed to keep a clear head for the next few hours. Whatever happened I must not appear *distraite*. And already time was passing.

Because of the many curtain calls and the crush leaving the Opera House we were late returning to the Residence. Guests who had not been at the ballet but whom I had invited to meet Anna de Lisle, had arrived. There was a certain amount of confusion. Although I had arranged for cloakrooms on the ground floor a couple of the women had gone upstairs and were looking for somewhere to put their furs. They were in the corridor that led only to Simon's rooms, and I redirected them.

I was close to his door when it opened and Simon came out.

'Where have you been?' I asked sharply, though the answer was obvious. 'What have you been doing?'

'I – I was just putting my programme away,' he said, startled by my vehemence. 'I didn't want it to get lost. Miss de Lisle autographed it for me.'

'I see.'

'You're all right, Lady Rayle?'

I hesitated. First Hugo and now Simon, I wasn't doing very well. 'Yes. I'm fine – except that I've got a splitting headache. I simply must take some aspirin. Be a dear, Simon, and cope for me till I get down, will you?'

It was a direct appeal, one that Simon could understand. Headaches were as old as Eve; his birds suffered from them at the most inconvenient times. He beamed his sympathy and hurried away to do my bidding.

I watched him go, then went through his sitting-room and into his bedroom. I turned the key in the cupboard-like door, switched on the light and went down the stairs. Wearing a long skirt I didn't find them easy to take. My heel caught in the hem and I nearly pitched forward. It reminded me of my arrival at Brussels National when I had fallen down the aircraft steps into the arms of Hugo and Simon and David Driscole. That seemed a long time ago now.

I had reached the bottom. I eased open the door and peered into the conservatory, where potted plants made darker shadows as the moon shone through the glass. There was a smell of damp growing things, of humus and fertilizer, and geraniums. It wasn't very warm. Beside me something stirred and there was a soft, positive pressure against my legs. I gave an involuntary gasp. But it was only the black and white tom, who was part of the establishment.

I bent to pick up the cat. He slipped away from me, however, and, praying that Baranov wouldn't fall over him and break a leg, I left him in the conservatory. Then I did what I had come to do; I made sure that the spring lock was fixed so that Baranov could hide at the top of the stairs outside Simon's bedroom until Anna came for him. He might have a long wait, in which case he would be uncomfortable and perhaps rather cold, but he ought to be safe. He had been instructed to lock the bottom door after him and I was going to lock the top door. Anna was afraid that he might get impatient and start wandering about the house. 'We have to remember that he is Baranov,' she said, as if this were self-explanatory.

I had fallen in with all of Anna's ideas. Dick Tindle had been short when I had finally managed to contact him. He had asked me abruptly if I were prepared to co-operate. If so, I must do what Anna advised, which included temporarily disregarding Simon's activities. But I was not to worry. Anna had his full support. 'We're depending on you, Catherine,' he had said. And I had capitulated, against my will.

The party was a kind of alibi. If asked, I could claim that I could hardly have been organizing a defection while entertaining a hundred guests. And the stairs to Simon's room had been an ideal solution to the problems of getting Baranov into the house during the party without encountering either guests or servants – ideal, that is, so long as Simon could be kept out of the way.

Once in the house, Baranov would spend the next day or two concealed in one of the guest suites. Anna would depart in the morning to visit her friends in the South of France and the servants would be told that she had left possessions in the suite which must not be disturbed. This would ensure Baranov's privacy, so that with my help and equipped with a picnic hamper and an electric kettle – not to mention the flowers and champagne and various delicacies that Anna had insisted on buying to welcome him – he should be able to survive not too uncomfortably. I hoped he would be appreciative.

Changing my torn skirt – at least this made an excellent excuse for my absence from the party – I told myself that I was being an uncharitable bitch. I had unlimited admiration for Baranov as a dancer. Why couldn't I feel more sympathy for him in his present predicament? Somehow I couldn't. His arrogant insistence on defecting where and how he chose struck me as being bloody selfish, as well as silly and unnecessary. The truth was that I wanted no part of the business. Whatever Dick Tindle's opinion of me might be I wasn't the stuff of which saints or heroines – or agents – are made.

But I could arrange a good party. Downstairs everything was going splendidly. Anna was receiving the guests, presented to her by Simon. The buffet was attracting attention and admiration. Champagne corks were giving that thick, satisfying plop which demonstrates that the bottle is being opened by an expert. The noise level in the room was just right, neither so high as to prevent pleasant conversation nor so low as to imply a dull gathering. And everybody seemed to be enjoying themselves.

Taking a glass of champagne, I moved from group to group. Daphne commented on my change of skirt. Hugo asked after my headache. The conversation was mainly about ballet and Baranov was constantly being mentioned; it was impossible to forget him. I collected some food on a plate, though I couldn't have felt less hungry, and drifted across to my French friends. Sir Thomas Bright, the British Ambassador to Belgium, was with them, and

Daphne and two or three others. I caught the end of a sentence, something about *Les Sylphides*.

'I've a very soft spot for *Les Sylphides*,' I said. 'For one thing it was the first ballet I ever saw. For another it was a memorable occasion because a sylph fell – we heard afterwards she had actually broken a bone – but the rest of the *corps* improvised, continued to dance round her and then carried her off as if it were meant to be. It was a marvellous performance in every way.'

I finished speaking and there was silence, one of those nasty, tight silences when everyone tries to think of the right thing to say until it is too late to say anything. Obviously I had put my foot in it somehow but I had no idea how. I had told this innocent little story scads of times but never had it got such a reception.

Daphne, who had been sitting on an arm of a sofa, broke the tension. She jumped to her feet and stood over me. 'You –' she said. 'You –' She was inarticulate with anger and there was a ghastly second when I thought she was going to throw the remains of her food at me. I sat, like a rabbit transfixed by a car's headlights, waiting for the inevitable.

'Daphne, my dear, what an extraordinary coincidence!' Sir Thomas said. 'Catherine, Daphne had just told us about that very incident – about the sylph falling and how wonderfully the *corps de ballet* coped with the situation. Evidently Hugo saw the same performance and has cherished the memory too. Isn't that strange?'

'Not strange at all,' Daphne said harshly. Her mouth was working as if she were getting ready to spit in my face. 'It's not the only thing that you and Hugo have shared, is it, Catherine?'

'Of course not. Hugo and I were contemporaries at Oxford,' I explained, 'years ago, while Daphne was still a child.' I forced myself to smile at her. 'The real coincidence is that I should have met Hugo again after – I hate to think how long.'

'And that he should be your – your second-in-command, Catherine. Yes. Yes, indeed,' the Ambassador said.

It could have been a light shining on his spectacles or it could have been an appreciative gleam in his eye but I would have sworn he winked at me. And his words had been a clear warning to Daphne. I recalled somebody telling me that H.E. didn't care what anybody did, providing they did it in a gentlemanly fashion, but scenes he couldn't abide. Though this was probably a *canard*, he had certainly helped out on this occasion; I was grateful.

Anyway, the whole incident was over in a matter of minutes and, one could only hope, forgotten. The party went on. The night wore into the morning. Guests began to leave. Hugo came to say goodbye and thank you. He looked harassed but it was nothing to do with me. My mind was on Baranov waiting at the top of the stairs outside Simon's bedroom.

At a quarter past one, as we had arranged, Anna made her apologies and, pleading her age and the excitement of the evening, said that she must retire. Simon insisted on seeing her to her room. I waited anxiously, wondering what I should do if he didn't return. But he came straight down again. Anna's departure had been taken as a signal so that the bulk of the guests were leaving. A hard core, however, still remained. I murmured to the houseman to serve the last round of drinks. At first the diplomatic habit of speeding the guest by withdrawing the liquor had appalled me; it would have been considered the height of bad manners in the Cotswolds, the equivalent of saying 'Time, gentlemen, please!' in one's own house. Now I was hardened to it. Nobody took offence. And it did have its uses.

By two o'clock everybody had gone. I said good night to Simon in the hall and, to my surprise, he thanked me profusely.

'That was a super evening, Lady Rayle, absolutely super. Thank you very much.'

'I'm glad you enjoyed it.'

I went upstairs, forcing myself to walk slowly when I was yearning to run, though I'm not sure where I wanted to run to. Baranov was such an unknown quantity. I hesitated before knocking on Anna's door.

When I opened it, the room was in darkness and one pair of curtains was drawn back. Anna, still dressed, was silhouetted against the window, staring into the garden. As I came in she turned sharply, drew the curtains and put on a bedside light. Her cheeks were hollowed, her eyes enormous.

'What is it?' I said. 'What's the matter?'

'He hasn't come,' she said. 'I went right down the stairs. I looked in the conservatory. There was a cat. It startled me. But no Baranov. Catherine, something must have gone wrong.'

Chapter 4

There was a burring noise in my ear. Somebody was shaking me. I grunted and turned on my back. But the noise had stopped, which was something to be thankful for. Sleep closed over me again.

'No, Hugo! No!'

I sat up with a jerk, wide awake. I had been dreaming of Hugo gently pouring champagne on to my face and into the hollow of my breasts. But it was Anna de Lisle, not Hugo, who was standing beside me in a dressing-gown.

'What is it?' I asked peevishly.

'It's six o'clock, Catherine, and the alarm has gone,' she said. 'We agreed – '

'I know.'

Because there was nothing else we could think of doing at half past two in the morning we had agreed that as soon as it was light I should make a search for Baranov. He might have arrived much later than we had expected and hidden somewhere. This seemed to me even less likely now than it had done before, but I couldn't back out.

I threw off the bedclothes and went into the bathroom. In five minutes I was dressed, in slacks, sweater, jacket and sneakers. I crept downstairs, feeling like a burglar in my own house.

Anna hadn't been able to remember if she had locked the bottom door of Simon's staircase. It was the first thing I tried and the latch was up. I didn't put on the light on the stairs. If Baranov, asleep on the top step, were suddenly awakened by the brightness, he might cry out and rouse Simon. Leaving the door open behind me I went cautiously upwards and peered around the last bend. There was no Baranov huddling in the shadows. I tiptoed down again and snicked shut the lock; in the unlikely event that I found him he wouldn't be entering the Residence that way.

I looked around the conservatory in a perfunctory fashion. Apart from the tom, who was snoring gently, there was nothing of interest. Which meant that there were only three possibilities; I really couldn't imagine Baranov curled up under a bush somewhere. But he could be in the gardener's shed or the greenhouse, which was heated, or – an outside chance – he might have found the folly in the middle of the maze. I tried the shed first and then the greenhouse.

It was when I was in the greenhouse that, glancing up from a collection of fertilizer sacks, I thought I glimpsed a dark shape merging into a tree-trunk. I stood still. Nothing happened. Nothing moved. And after a couple of minutes I gave up and set off for the maze. By now I was sure that Baranov was nowhere in the grounds, but I couldn't ignore the last possibility. I had to satisfy Anna. I walked fast, eager to make an end of this stupid search. Footsteps followed me. I stopped, holding my breath and telling myself that I must have been mistaken. The footsteps stopped too, but not quite quickly enough. I went on until I reached the entrance of the maze, and then whipped round. There was no one in sight and nothing stirred. This was becoming absurd.

Before I left the house I had picked up one of Guy's old sticks. It was made from a cabbage stalk – he had bought it on a holiday in Jersey – and it was a heavy, knobbly affair, a good weapon. It gave me some confidence. Grasping it firmly I went into the maze.

The maze was small and simple. The key to the centre was left, right, left; left, right, left; and so on. In the centre was the folly, best described as a wooden gazebo, except that it had no view apart from the encircling hedges. During the summer it might be a pleasant place to come and read but now, very early on a late autumn morning, it was cold and claustrophobic. I shivered. Baranov was lucky not to have spent the night there.

I started back, thinking of hot coffee and another hour in bed. Close beside me but on the other side of a hedge someone sneezed. The sound, though muffled, was unmistakable. I froze.

The sound was repeated, less loud, more agonized as the sneezer sought to subdue it. I turned and fled.

Thankful for my sneakers, I ran almost noiselessly. Right, left, right. Right, left, right. Right, left, and I turned to find myself at a dead end. I stood, my heart thudding, my breathing much too loud. I was lost in the damned maze. And I was pretty certain that whoever was in there with me wasn't Baranov.

The one thing not to do was panic. If I kept my head and retraced my steps – left, right, left – I should come to the place where I had heard the sneeze and where I must have gone wrong. With a bit of luck I could start again. But I had no luck. Around the third or fourth corner I ran slap into him. Simultaneously I recognized Simon and raised the stick, prepared to hit him. He seized my arm and wrenched the stick from me. I brought my knee up into his crutch. He staggered back, releasing my arm, and swore at me with a wealth of vocabulary I wouldn't have suspected he possessed.

'Simon!'

I wasn't nearly as surprised as I pretended to be. After all, he was the obvious person to be flitting around the grounds of the Residence. The knee in his crutch had been more a punishment for the earlier fright he had given me than an act of self-preservation. But he could scarcely complain. If he were going to spy on me he had to take the consequences.

'Simon!' I said again, keeping my face straight with an effort. 'My dear boy, whatever are you doing here? I hope I haven't done you any lasting damage.'

He was holding himself between the legs like a small boy. He gritted his teeth. 'I'll live,' he said. 'Thank you, Lady Rayle.' He began to massage himself.

Eventually I gave him Guy's stick and he went off to have a final look round for the suspicious character we both said we had seen in the garden. I went back to Anna. She received my news stoically; she'd had little hope that I would find Baranov. She insisted, however, that he might still come.

'Anna, isn't there any means of getting in touch with the people who were to deliver him?'

'No,' she said tartly. 'Don't you understand, Catherine?

Yesterday my contact was to be at a certain public telephone at a certain time. He was. I gave him the information he needed. He failed to deliver Baranov as instructed. Something must have gone wrong. Well, he's not going to sit around by that phone waiting for me to call, is he?'

'What will he do?'

'Contact you. He knows where Baranov was meant to come. That is, if there's a hope in heaven left of delivering him.'

I hid my frustration. 'So you'll be staying on for a day or two in case – '

Anna shook her head. 'No, there's nothing more I can do here. It's better to keep to the original plan and go on to my friends in Hyères. We'll have to hope there'll be good news of Baranov soon. Until then you'd better keep his door locked and the servants out as we arranged. I'll be in touch with Dick.'

'But, Anna – ' My frustration had turned to consternation.

She patted me on the arm. 'You'll manage, my dear. Just take care.'

Take care! I had come to Brussels to the NATO Council to do a specific job for which, God knows, I wasn't really qualified. I was the Lady Amateur. Nevertheless, according to Sir Richard Tindle, I hadn't been doing too badly. Now, suddenly and without warning, I was plunged into the middle of a completely extraneous mess that had nothing to do with me. And I was way out of my depth. It was no bloody use telling me to 'take care'.

I sat in my place at the doughnut-shaped table in the Council chamber and half listened through my ear-phones. It was a little easier to understand the English simultaneous translation of the Turkish Permanent Representative's speech than it was to understand his broken French. But either the interpreter was having an off-day or the Turk was growing confused. The sentences were becoming more and more convoluted, the meaning more and more obscure. I could feel my head begin to nod; it had been a very short night. I took off the ear-phones and looked at my papers. I was due to speak next.

The Turk droned on. Beside me, the American Permrep was muttering to himself. Like most NATO bodies, the Council is very casual by international standards: interruptions and questions are usually permitted. But today for some reason the Secretary General was in a bad temper and had quashed an effort by my United States colleague to intervene. Undoubtedly he would have something to say when the Turk had finished. After that it would be my turn.

I frowned over my notes. We were discussing force reductions in Europe – an item that had been on almost every Council agenda since I had taken my place. I intended to follow my usual line: there was no diminution of the threat; the future was uncertain; if NATO dropped its guard, Germany, Austria, the whole of Europe could be endangered.

The Turk wound down his peroration and, as I had predicted, the American made his objections. A hand appeared over my shoulder, a piece of paper under my nose. It read: 'Your Excellency is wanted on the telephone by a friend of Dick's.'

I had spent the day expecting and fearing some such message. Now it had come, at a most awkward moment. There was no time to think. It had to be one of those instant decisions. I swivelled in my seat so that I could look Hugo in the face.

'Tell him to ring back in an hour,' I whispered.

'Certainly,' Hugo whispered back, scribbling a hasty note that he handed to the messenger. Seemingly as an after-thought he added: 'I suppose I couldn't take the call for you?'

'No, thank you,' I said. 'It's a personal matter.'

'The United Kingdom, Lady Rayle!' the Secretary General said, with a touch of impatience.

I apologized and looked around at the blank benign ambassadors, backed by their minions. The boredom of the rows of faces, all male, told me that they knew precisely what the Lady Amateur was going to say. For a mad moment I was tempted to confound them by announcing that the world-famous Baranov intended to defect – if he hadn't changed his mind. That would have set them alight. Prudence, however, prevailed and I began my set speech. If they were not interested in the dangers that faced the Western Alliance, they damned well should have been.

Forty minutes later, having handed over to Hugo, I was back in my office waiting for the telephone to ring and cursing Anna de Lisle for not having delayed her departure by one day at least. Then the call came through, exactly on time, which was reassuring. It reminded me that I was dealing with professionals.

''Allo! Lady Rayle? Yes?'

'Yes. I'm Catherine Rayle.'

'Good. I'm a friend of Dick's. You understand?'

'Yes. Wait a moment, please.'

My phone had an extension in Simon's office. If Simon was proposing to listen to my conversation, I could disappoint him. I could easily send him on an errand. I jerked open the door to his room.

Simon, his fair head bent over his papers, was concentrated on some draft or other he was writing. He looked up, seemingly startled.

'Lady Rayle – is something wrong?'

'No. But I want some files, in a hurry.'

'Of course. You have the numbers? I'll send for them right away.'

I dictated half a dozen numbers and Simon jotted them down on a pad of paper. At least two of the files were already on my desk so he would have trouble finding them. I could apologize later.

'Go along to the Registry and get them yourself, will you? It'll be quicker and I want them at once.'

Whether or not he had intended to eavesdrop Simon had enough sense not to quibble. He did as he had been told and, leaving the connecting door open so that I would see anyone who came into his room, I returned to the telephone.

'Sorry to keep you waiting. I wanted to make sure we weren't overheard.'

'That is good. All the same, we shall talk as circumspectly as possible, Lady Rayle. I will explain to you and you will explain to my friend, Dick. That way he does not blame us. Listen carefully now.'

He began to speak very rapidly and, from his voice and accent – he pronounced every 'i' as if it were a double 'e' – I pictured him, dark, sallow, greasy, ready to pimp his sisters; I couldn't imagine him as any friend that Dick would ever have.

And his apparent self-importance mixed with nervousness gave me little confidence.

'It was bad, very bad. Everything went wrong, which was a pity because it was not a difficult operation,' he said. 'Last night, after the performance, they take B in a limousine from the theatre to the Embassy where he is staying. There is a chauffeur and a bodyguard. We have two cars. One drives across their bows, stops them. They try to reverse but our other car is behind. It is late. We have chosen a narrow quiet street. With four of us we highpower the chauffeur and bodyguard and drive off with B. Everybody – except the Russians – is happy and nobody is hurt. That was the plan. It didn't work.'

'Was – someone hurt?'

'The Russians wouldn't stop. They tried to drive through our car. It was a big confusion.'

'Was B hurt? Tell me what happened.' I heard the rising panic in my voice. 'Where is he? Is he all right?'

'He was knocked out so he couldn't help himself. We had to fight to get him out of the Russians' car. There were two of them hanging on to him and two of us. The numbers were not on our side after all. We started at only three because a man was ill and did not come. Then the Captain hit his head on the windscreen, when the cars crashed. But we fought, we fought like lions.' He paused as if doubtful what to say next. 'And we beat them. The Captain, in spite of his hurt, came to help us. He is very strong.' He stopped again and this time I was sure that something was worrying him. 'Very strong,' he repeated, to reassure either himself or me.

'Go on,' I said grimly.

'If only we had remembered their driver – ' He sighed. 'We had almost reached our car when he started to shoot. We all dived for cover, except B. B was dazed, confused. He didn't know where he was. He began to run back to the Russians and was hit.'

'Hit! Shot, you mean? Oh God!' I was appalled. 'He's not – not – '

'No, no! The wound is painful but not serious.'

'But – what did you do? Did you take him to the hospital?'

'We are not fools!' he said contemptuously. 'We got away, safely, all of us. And we have B. Soon – in a day or two – he will be delivered to you, if – if everything goes well.'

At least they had had the sense not to deliver him last night. I had a vision of Baranov crouched outside Simon's bedroom door, bleeding and half-conscious. What on earth would Anna and I have done?

'I'm glad you didn't bring him straight to the Residence,' I said.

'It was not possible,' he said. 'I had not been given the instructions where to deliver him.'

'But – ' I said, 'I don't understand. You must have had them. You were told precisely what to do. B was to be brought to the Residence through the conservatory and – '

'I know now, Lady Rayle. I know now. Then only the Captain knew and there were other things to be done first.'

'What things?'

He didn't answer. Instead he said: 'I must go. I will telephone you again when it is time for the delivery.'

'Wait a minute. You haven't told me where B is or – '

'Soon, I telephone, soon. Goodbye, Lady Rayle.'

'Wait!'

He murmured something I didn't catch and the line went dead. I stared at the instrument in disbelief. Slowly I put back the receiver.

The most famous ballet dancer in the world had been concussed and fought over and shot at, and was now being hidden somewhere in Brussels until he could be delivered to me. And the Russians . . . My mind balked. I began to laugh. It was a fantastic situation.

Chapter 5

I was in the bath, trying to relax, when Anna telephoned the following evening. It had been a very nervous day. I had failed to get in touch with Dick, who seemed to be abroad again, and so far there had been no word from his so-called friend. From worrying about how I was to cope with Baranov, I had gone on to worry about Baranov himself. I wished I knew how badly he had been wounded and how well he was being cared for; words like septicæmia kept occurring to me, to be thrust to the back of my mind. I told myself that Baranov wasn't my responsibility, not yet, but that didn't help much.

Anna was on the phone. I wrapped myself in a bath-towel and took the call in my bedroom. I thought of my French friends who were about to take me to the Bolshoi in the expectation of seeing Baranov dance. It wasn't going to be an easy party.

'Catherine, my dear,' Anna said, 'I so enjoyed my visit to you.' She spent one, two minutes chatting before she came to the point. 'That present from Dick, has it arrived?'

'No.' I hesitated, remembering that Simon could easily be listening to our conversation. 'It's on the way. It got damaged in transit and has to be repaired.'

There was a perceptible pause before Anna answered. 'But the delivery people have contacted you? Did they say when you would get it?'

'Yes. I heard from them yesterday. They said it would be delivered in a day or two, if – if all went well. But, Anna – '

'Good,' she said. 'That's wonderful news.'

And, before I could frame a suitable explanation of the situation that would both enlighten Anna and baffle Simon, Anna had said how pleased Dick would be, after all the trouble he had taken choosing the present, and rung off. She left me feeling angry, with her and myself. She had got the wrong impression. She believed – and would doubtless tell Dick, if she could get hold of him – that everything was splendid, whereas in fact the reverse was true. It was my fault, of course; I was stupid at double-talk. But she could have shown more patience and not been quite so insouciant.

I finished drying myself, dressed and went downstairs. Coffee and sandwiches had been put in the drawing-room. As the Belgian Government was giving a reception for the Bolshoi after the ballet this was my dinner. I hadn't intended to share it with Simon.

'I thought Mrs Pewter was having a party for the Nuclear Planners this evening,' I said pointedly.

'Yes, she is, Lady Rayle.' He gave me a winning smile. 'But – I was tempted by your sandwiches.'

I accepted the half-truth and wondered what he really wanted. He didn't seem to want anything, not even the sandwiches. He ate very slowly and sipped the coffee as if he needed to make it last. He twice looked at his watch.

'You mustn't be late,' I said.

'Nor must you, Lady Rayle,' he said. 'I do envy you seeing the Bolshoi again. They were super on Tuesday. Last night, according to the papers, their performance of *Sleeping Beauty* was frightful and Baranov danced atrociously.'

'What?' I croaked, my mouth full of sandwich. I had been terribly busy all day and, although I had skimmed the headlines to see if the news of Baranov's disappearance had broken yet, it literally hadn't occurred to me to wonder how the ballet company might be managing without him.

'I know. It sounds improbable, doesn't it? Evidently he stumbled a couple of times and once almost dropped Aurora. The audience gasped. He was as awful as that.'

It didn't merely sound improbable; it was impossible. Baranov hadn't danced atrociously because he hadn't danced at all. He had been lying in some hidden room with a bullet wound in his body. I had no intention, however, of telling Simon that!

I decided it was time to go. Simon insisted on seeing me to the front door and helping me into the car. Glancing out of the rear window as we purred down the drive, I saw that he had gone back into the house. Obviously he was in no hurry to get to the Pewters' party; Daphne would not be pleased.

But that was no concern of mine. My thoughts returned inevitably to Baranov and the unfortunate *premier danseur* who must have danced in his place. I wondered if Simon had exaggerated the awfulness of his performance. But when I got to the Théâtre Royal I found that my French friends too were full of the story, and we speculated about how badly Baranov would dance tonight. It was an effort for me to make the right noises in response.

I studied my programme. Baranov was billed to dance in *Pas de Deux* and scenes from *Carmen* – the first half of the performance – but not in *The Liberators*, 'a modern Russian ballet with a political theme', which took up the second half. There was no slip in the programme to say that he would be unable to appear and no announcement before the curtain went up.

Baranov appeared. The *Pas de Deux* was a show piece. He danced it beautifully, with great finesse. He was – tremendous! In *Carmen*, technically less difficult, he was not quite as good, or so I thought. Perhaps I was being hypercritical. The audience, convinced that they were watching the great Baranov, were enraptured, and whoever the dancer was, he had certainly redeemed the débâcle of the previous night.

I focused my opera-glasses on his face as he received a final ovation. He didn't look unlike Baranov but then I, like ninety-five per cent of the audience, didn't really know what Baranov looked like. All photographs showed him in costume and theatrical make-up. Which, I presumed, was why the Russians had twice been able to get away with a substitute. But why, I asked myself, had they made the effort? Was it to buy time? They couldn't hope to sit on the story of Baranov's disappearance for long. And, if it were to buy time, what were they doing with it? Were they using it to try to find their lost compatriot? The worrying questions ruined any enjoyment I might have had from the second half of the programme.

It was almost a relief to say goodbye to my friends, who were not invited to the Belgian reception. I envied them. I would much rather have gone home to bed. But an hour or less of doing my duty and, I promised myself, I should be on my way.

At the Palais des Congrès I gave up my coat, signed the book, and queued to be announced. We shuffled slowly forward. The reception line was very long and there was some sort of hold-up.

'*Non, non, non, mademoiselle!*' an anguished voice said. 'You may not kiss Monsieur Baranov. It is not allowed.'

A girl laughed, protested in an American accent, said she was his greatest fan. Her male companion, embarrassed, hurried her along. We began to move again. I shook hands with a Belgian who meant nothing to me, the Bolshoi ballet master, the *prima ballerina* who had danced the *Pas de Deux* – and Baranov. It was a traumatic experience.

The *prima ballerina* smiled at me with her mouth only. 'Comrade Baranov' didn't smile at all. The comrade had dark hair, dark eyes, high cheekbones and a pale, pointed face, the same face that I had seen earlier in the evening through my opera-glasses. This was the *premier danseur* who had danced the *Pas de Deux* and *Carmen*. I was astounded. It had never occurred to me that the Russians would have the audacity to pass him off as Baranov at an international reception. No wonder he looked ill and exhausted. To dance as Baranov must have been a terrible strain but to impersonate him in public was surely much worse. It was ludicrous that the Russians should make him take such a wild risk.

Then the obvious but totally unacceptable explanation occurred to me and I shied away from it.

We were shaking hands. Comrade Baranov's face was impassive. His large, bruised-looking eyes gazed over my shoulder into the middle distance. He couldn't have been less interested. But his index finger was pressing what felt like a piece of thickly folded paper into my palm.

And I found myself clutching a note from a supposed Baranov in a hand that another Russian, whom I suspected at once of being KGB, was waiting to shake. His arm was already extending itself towards me. Half mesmerized, I would have passed on the note to him. I didn't know what to do with it. I had no pockets. My blouse was high-necked, my sleeves tight. My evening bag had a complicated clasp and, anyway, was too obvious. My mouth . . . I couldn't swallow the damned thing. I had to read it.

Nearby there was a metallic thud as if a gong had been mis-hit. This was followed by a much louder thud as somebody fell to the floor. I turned to see a shower of champagne, glasses, tray describing a parabola in the air. There were cries of dismay as guests were splattered with the liquid and a much louder scream from a woman hit on the shoulder by the flying tray; broken glass crunched underfoot.

In the ensuing confusion I had just enough presence of mind to transfer the little wad of paper from my right hand to my left.

Hugo Pewter, CMG, United Kingdom Deputy Permanent Representative to the North Atlantic Council, picked himself gingerly off the floor. I caught the word *ivre*, but Hugo was not drunk. Hugo had had an accident – at a most opportune moment for me.

'I am most frightfully sorry,' he said, in a general apology. 'I slipped on the floor and must have kicked the tray from underneath. I do apologize. I hope nobody was hurt.' He limped across to the woman who had been hit by the tray. *'Madame, mes excuses. Je suis désolé . . .'*

There was a murmur of sympathy for Hugo before the guests returned to their conversations. Servants were already hurrying to sweep up the débris. The incident was over. I turned back to the reception line and completed my hand-shaking.

I made my way purposefully to the buffet, bowing to one or two acquaintances but not stopping to talk. I asked for champagne and put the glass on the table. Then I opened my bag, extracted a wisp of cambric, dabbed at my nose and replaced the handkerchief – together with the note that had been burning my left hand. My curiosity would have to wait.

It waited longer than I had intended but I didn't want to be among the first to leave the reception. Besides, I had some difficulty in cornering the wife of the Canadian Counsellor, who had not only danced with the Royal Winnipeg Ballet before her marriage but had recently arrived in Brussels from a posting in the USSR. I was sure that while she was in Moscow she would have seen Baranov dance and I hoped that she had met him. I could think of no one else who might tell me what I needed to know.

Fortunately she was a bright, vivacious woman, who was happy to talk about the ballet. She told me that she had visited the Bolshoi innumerable times in Moscow and thought that nobody in the world could compare with Baranov. She hadn't yet seen him dance in Brussels but she had tickets for *Sleeping Beauty* and was looking forward to it, more than she could say.

At least this gave me an opening. 'You were lucky your tickets weren't for yesterday. I gather he danced very badly.'

'So I heard. The poor man must have been unwell. That's the only explanation, Lady Rayle. Of course, it was a tragedy for the audience.'

'I thought it might have been an – an understudy.' I wondered how on earth I could get her to answer the unaskable question. 'I mean, if he had looked like Baranov, nobody in the audience would have known, would they? For that matter I rather doubt if more than a handful of people at this reception could be positive that it is Baranov to whom they've just been introduced.'

She looked at me oddly, then shifted her gaze to my empty champagne glass. 'That's Baranov all right,' she said sharply. 'I can assure you of that, Lady Rayle.'

'Of course you would know.' I gave her a sycophantic smile. 'But few Westerners would. Our press never seems to publish close-ups of his face. I can't think why. He's quite handsome.'

'Well, the Russian press does,' she said. 'His face is famous in the USSR. And that's Baranov, Lady Rayle. I promise you. I've met him on several occasions. He's even given me his autograph for my daughter.'

'Oh, I never actually doubted it, not for a minute,' I lied, and asked her about the Winnipeg Ballet.

After a decent interval I said I must go but I hoped she and her husband would dine with me soon; I owed her a good dinner for the information she had given me, shattering as it was. I thanked the Belgian Minister for Cultural Affairs and his wife, said good night to a few people, collected my coat and had almost reached the hall when someone came running down the marble stairs behind me.

'Catherine!'

Damn Hugo! If he had anything to say to me he could have said it during the reception, but it so happened we hadn't spoken. I had no desire to chat to him now. 'Yes?' I said, unwelcomingly.

'Would you be good enough to give me a lift to the Residence? Simon dropped me off on his way somewhere and I haven't any transport.'

'Yes, of course.' I couldn't refuse; Baranov's note would have to stay unread a little longer. 'You're still limping,' I said, as we went across the hall.

'Yes, I must have pulled a muscle.' Hugo smiled. 'The next time I need to create a diversion I must do something less spectacular.'

I didn't ask him what he meant. I said: 'I'll get Rule to take you home first.'

'No, don't do that,' he said. 'I'm hoping you'll offer me a night-cap.'

'I'm sorry, Hugo, but it's rather late.'

'Oh, please!'

'Won't Daphne be waiting for you?'

'No. She said she was exhausted after the party for the Planners and was going straight to bed.'

'Well, I'm tired too,' I said firmly. 'So you'll have to forgive me.'

'Personally, my dear Ambassador,' he said, 'I'd forgive you anything. But –' he leaned towards me and murmured in my ear – 'the Russians won't. They take a dim view of people who help their nationals to defect.'

I didn't know what to say. Hugo might have been guessing but it was a reasoned guess. He didn't merely suspect my interest in Baranov. It hadn't been an accident that he had kicked over the tray of champagne immediately after Baranov had pressed that folded piece of paper into my hand; he had deliberately distracted attention from me. Suddenly I felt enormously relieved. There were a lot of reasons why I couldn't have told Hugo about Baranov, but if he already knew . . .

We came out of the Palais des Congrès into the flood-lighting. Rule opened the door of the Rolls and Hugo got in beside me.

'If you really want it,' I said, 'you can have a whole bottle of Moët et Chandon.'

He didn't respond. 'I would prefer tea,' he said austerely, 'with milk.'

Somewhat chastened, I shut my eyes and pretended to doze. Hugo showed no inclination to disturb me. I tried to make my mind a blank. Baranov was a practical problem. I could reach no decisions until I had read his note. To expect it to say, 'I've changed my mind. I don't want to go to Israel after all. Thank you. B.' was mere wishful-thinking.

In fact it read: 'I come tomorrow after First Act. Have car ready. Drive by stage door at once the cat leaves. Make sure no more mistakes.' And it was an order, not a request.

The note, much wrinkled from being folded into such a small wad, lay on the kitchen table and Hugo was smoothing it compulsively with his thumb. I was hovering by the cooker, waiting for the kettle to boil. I had already laid a tray with tea-things. Our conversation, however, was not exactly in keeping with the domesticity of the scene.

'He should be shot!' Hugo said vehemently.

'Who?'

'Dick Tindle,' Hugo said. 'He deserves it. He ought never to have got you mixed up in this cloak-and-dagger business.'

'He didn't really mean to,' I said.

'Oh, don't be a fool, Kit.' Hugo seized the tray from me and stalked into the drawing-room. Over his shoulder he said: 'Tindle never does anything he doesn't mean. He's the most devious character one can imagine.' He put down the tray and waited while I poured. 'Now,' he said, after he had sipped his tea, 'tell me all, from the moment Tindle propositioned you.' And when I hesitated he added gently: 'You must, Kit. You haven't any option. You need help if Baranov's to be picked up tomorrow. There's no time for Tindle to fix it.'

I told Hugo everything I could remember, beginning with my first meeting with Dick Tindle beside Guy's grave. He was an attentive listener. Two or three times he wanted a point elucidated but mostly he was content to nod his head as if I were confirming what he already knew.

When I came to the end he said: 'Good God, they did make a balls-up of it, didn't they? No wonder Baranov's note was so snippy about mistakes. But what I'd like to know – the most important thing – is why he went back to the Bolshoi, how he managed it and when, and what he told his comrades after he got back. It doesn't make sense to me.' Hugo finished his tea and held out his cup. 'More, please. I suppose – Kit, this character who calls himself a friend of Dick's, do you think his account of what happened is reliable?'

I shrugged. 'It's difficult to judge just from a voice. He could have easily exaggerated everything. Perhaps Baranov wasn't shot. Perhaps the bullet just creased his arm or his shoulder. That would at least explain how he was able to dance.'

'Yes,' Hugo said doubtfully. 'Kit, you do appreciate that this set-up for tomorrow night may be a trap, don't you? Baranov may have no intention of defecting, not any more.'

'What sort of trap?'

'I don't know, but doubtless I shall find out.'

'Oh no!' I said. 'No, Hugo! You're not going anywhere near that theatre tomorrow. Anna de Lisle said Dick Tindle didn't want anyone else from the Mission involved.'

'My dear Kit, I've been involved in this affair from the start. Surely you've realized that? Or do you think I spy on all my ambassadors as I've spied on you? For God's sake, you must have suspected Simon. Kit – what is it?'

'N – nothing.'

The curtains of one of the french windows had not been properly drawn and, glancing up, I had had a sudden impression of a face, a figure standing behind the glass. It must have been a movement of the climbing rose or the reflection of the moon as the clouds passed. I was tired and jumpy and now I was imagining things.

'What did you mean about you being involved from the start?' I said.

'Well, very soon after your husband died, a chap I know in the Office turned up in Brussels for some meeting or other.

He just happened to mention the name of Rayle and took the opportunity to sound out my feelings for you.' Hugo grinned at me. Over the weeks we had become friends again in the easy way of people who had once known each other intimately, but this was the first reference he had made to our previous relationship. 'I told him that twenty years was a long time but I wished you well – with all my heart.

'He also mentioned that, although I had been more or less promised it, I was unlikely to get the top job here. Some political appointee would probably replace the then ambassador. These two items, I might say, were not juxtaposed and at the time it never occurred to me that you or any woman could be a possible Permrep.

'Later I was summoned to London and given the score. I was to keep the boat steady and pointed in the right direction. You were to be the figurehead on the prow. Political reasons, I was informed.'

'Political reasons? But what's political about Baranov?'

'I don't know, Kit. But there's something more behind all this than a ballet dancer, even if it is the great Baranov, and it must be something pretty important. Incidentally, nobody mentioned any guff about Jeanne d'Arc leading a crusade for NATO – not, of course, that poor old NATO doesn't need it.' Hugo stopped abruptly; he must have seen my expression. 'Sorry, Kit. But we might as well be honest, mightn't we?'

'Yes,' I said, 'if you're sure you're right, that it was always Baranov who was important to Dick. But, if so, why bring me into it? I might be just credible as a second Joan of Arc, but he could scarcely have found a less acceptable James Bond.'

Hugo laughed. 'You can say that again,' he said. 'I could imagine you waiting for Baranov at the stage door tomorrow night – in the Rolls, with Rule chauffeuring you.'

'It makes a nice picture,' I admitted.

'Ah well, you've prepared the guest suite very adequately. Or was that Anna de Lisle's work?'

'What?'

'Simon burgled it this evening after you had gone to the ballet.

He reports that if Baranov doesn't come soon you'll need some new flowers.'

'Thank you.'

'You mustn't blame Simon. He's been very useful. And I had to be sure what you were up to.'

'Why? Tell me, Hugo, if it had been someone else – some other political appointee, and not me – would you have arranged for Simon to live in the Residence and listen to my phone calls and report on my movements and whatever?'

'My dear Kit,' he mocked me. 'In the normal course of events I would have kept well away and let you or whoever it was get on with his politicking. I don't believe in looking for trouble. But when I was warned that the new Permrep was to be a protégé of Dick Tindle's, whose machinations I know only too well, and then the protégé turned out to be you, I had to find out what was going on – for self-preservation. It's as simple as that. Remember, Kit, if you or Tindle foul up the UK Mission it's my career that'll suffer, not yours.'

I nodded. I wondered if Dick had foreseen, or even intended, Hugo's reaction. It could be the reason he had picked on me. I felt deflated. I had been a fool to –

There it was again, a shimmering of light between the curtains, and a white face pressed against the glass. I hadn't moved my head this time, only my eyes, but for a moment I had seen the face distinctly. Somebody was standing on the flower-bed and staring into the drawing-room, somebody small, to judge from the position of the head, and slight.

'Kit, are you listening?'

'There's somebody watching us from outside.'

'What?'

Hugo didn't attempt any finesse. He twisted around, pushed himself out of the sofa and made for the window. He fumbled with the locks.

'Turn out the damned lights.'

I did as I was told, then felt my way over to him. He had the window open by now and we both peered into the darkness. There was nothing to be seen, but I thought I heard the sound of running footsteps. It was impossible to be sure; the wind was fitful and rain was beginning to fall. A sudden squall blew drops of water over us, driving us back into the room. Hugo shut the windows, locked them and drew the curtains carefully.

'There was no one there,' he said. 'You imagined it, Kit.'

'Perhaps.'

I wasn't prepared to argue, not even when Hugo repeated his statement. He didn't sit down again; instead he walked backwards and forwards between the sofa and the windows. Suddenly he said it was terribly late and we must get some sleep, and anyway nothing could be done till morning.

It was raining hard now and I had to lend him an umbrella. I gave him time to get up the hill, then I once more opened the window. I knelt inside the room and leant over the lintel to inspect with the help of a torch the flower-bed below. If someone had been standing there, the footprints would be clear in the damp earth. There were no footprints. But the ground looked roughly raked, as if by the ferrule of an umbrella. Which convinced me that Hugo had caught a glimpse of the face and guessed, as I had, that the watcher was Daphne.

Chapter 6

By the next morning, which was Friday, I had forgotten about Daphne. There were more important things to think about, specifically Baranov. He dominated my thoughts throughout the day – he and the rain.

The rain went on and on, until everything was sodden, easing only in the evening as we were setting out from the Residence. Simon, who had earlier made an abject apology for having kept me 'under surveillance', held an umbrella over me as I folded myself into his MG. Then he came around the back of the car, contracted his length with practised ease into the driving seat and slammed the door. But he didn't start the engine.

'Lady Rayle, are you sure you won't change your mind? The odds are we'll pick up Baranov and bring him straight back here without any fun and games. But – '

'It's because of that "but" I'm coming with you, Simon,' I said firmly.

I wasn't going to argue about it any more. Much as I had disliked the idea, I had been forced to leave all the arrangements for collecting Baranov to Hugo and Simon. I couldn't cope myself, and I had not been able to contact Dick Tindle; I had tried, but all I had got was his deputy who repeated that Dick was out of the country and had left no messages. Nevertheless, I was determined to share the responsibility and, where Hugo had failed to persuade me to stay at home, Simon could scarcely have hoped to succeed; this must have been a last-ditch attempt. Now he accepted defeat gracefully, only allowing himself a gusty sigh before flicking the ignition switch.

The engine fired at once and we shot off down the drive. Water spurted from under our wheels. At the entrance he braked sharply. Then we rocketed into the road and I held on to my seat, hoping that he wouldn't notice. It was a change from my usual sedate progress in the Rolls.

The drive into Brussels was without incident. Simon avoided the main boulevards ringing the city and instead chose to wind his way into the old part of Brussels, the Ilot Sacré. Several times he looked at his watch and seemed to adjust his route accordingly. It was not unlike a rally. We were due to arrive at an appointed spot at an appointed time. At H-hour precisely we arrived. Unfortunately there was nowhere to park.

We drove around and around, gradually taking in more streets. I could feel Simon's growing tension; but he continued to be choosy. Twice he turned down perfectly good parking places that I had pointed out to him. The third time this happened, in the Rue de Bouchers, I wanted to know why.

'Because I could easily be stuck there,' he said. 'I must be able to get away at speed, Lady Rayle. A contingency plan that won't work isn't much use, is it?'

Personally I didn't see the need for a contingency plan, not if our main plan wasn't going to get off the ground. At this rate we would never arrive at the Théâtre Royal de la Monnaie. And Baranov wouldn't be able to wait for us. After the disaster that Dick's people had contrived he couldn't be expected to take any more risks; he must already be suspect and closely watched. God knows what might happen to him if again he tried to defect and failed. I was about to say all this when Simon jammed on the brakes and I narrowly avoided going through the windscreen.

By now we were back in the Rue de Persil and Simon had seen what he considered the ideal parking place. It was, however, on the opposite side of the street. He swung the MG in a U-turn, which he couldn't make in one. Obstructing the traffic in both directions, he reversed and had another go. The second time he was successful and we glided happily into the gutter, but not before there had been a lot of hooting and the shrill of a police whistle. Simon swore.

We had been unlucky again. The gendarme leant his bicycle against a lamp standard and stood over the MG. He said nothing. He waited for us to get reluctantly out of the car. He couldn't have helped seeing our CD plates, but Brussels abounds with diplomats of one kind or another and he must have had his fill of them. Even so, if he had been going off to his supper, he would probably have ignored us; as it was, he had to be coming on duty, because he was happy to waste ten minutes inspecting our passports, our *cartes d'identité* and the car's papers, before dismissing us with a reprimand.

'Come on, Lady Rayle,' Simon said sharply, almost before the gendarme had cocked his leg over his saddle.

Simon turned into a narrow, badly-lit entrance that would have been easy to miss, and set off between the shops. As an arcade it didn't compare with the Galerie Toison d'Or or the Galerie Louise but another time I would have enjoyed browsing there. Now, thirty yards and, in spite of my long legs, I was almost running to keep up with Simon, when he suddenly dived through a slit between a *charcuterie* and a lace-maker's and came out on a main street. Parked at the kerb was a two-door Mercedes. Hugo was standing beside it.

'Where the hell have you been?' he said.

'There was nowhere to – ' Simon began.

'Get in,' Hugo said. 'In the back, both of you. Move across, Kit. And hurry! We're running late.'

I scrambled over the seat. Simon, pressing behind me, was both a help and a hindrance. I collapsed in my corner as Hugo slammed the car door and drove off. Simon nearly fell on top of me.

When we had settled ourselves, Simon said: 'You got a coupé, I see. That was a pity, Hugo. It won't be so easy. Baranov'll have to get in without help and he'll be slow. He'll slow everything.'

'Then we'll have to be quicker,' Hugo said, 'if necessary. And don't complain, Simon. This is a damn good car, fast, easy to handle and not traceable to us. If you ask me I was lucky. I might have got worse – or none at all.'

'Where did you get it?' I asked. 'You didn't steal it, I hope.

'No, Kit!' He didn't laugh. 'I don't believe in breaking the law, at least if I can avoid it. I got the car through a friend, who has been altogether very helpful.'

'She's fixed the garage?'

'Yes, Simon.'

'What garage?'

'For God's sake!' Hugo said. 'This is for real. I've done the best I could. I've taken some minor precautions in case things go wrong. Now, please, shut up, both of you. We're almost there.'

We drove past the peristyled front of the Théâtre Royal de la Monnaie, which had that hushed and secret mien theatres acquire when a live performance is taking place inside. Tonight the performance was *Giselle*, given by the Bolshoi Ballet Company with Baranov dancing Albrecht – for the first act only.

This, as Hugo said, was for real. It wasn't the mad dream that it seemed to me or the high adventure I suspected Simon half-fancied it was. My insides churned. I thought of Dick Tindle. Maybe I should have explained everything to his deputy, but he hadn't given me much chance. He'd been so bloody patronizing. Now it was too late. We were committed. We had to see the thing through – if we could.

Hugo said: 'And here we sit for five, ten minutes, watching that door twenty-odd yards along there on the right and praying hard to St Michael and Ste Gudule. And before either of you asks me who they are, I'll tell you. They're the patron saints of Brussels, so they should be prepared to help us not to scandalize their city. Remember, scandal is anathema to Her Majesty's Foreign and Commonwealth Office, and we're a pretty vulnerable car-load.'

He was still chatting and making us chat, lowering the tension, when we heard the applause. We were parked in a patch of shadow beside the wall of the opera house and the noise seemed to grow out of the ground and shake the building. It shook us too, even Hugo, who stopped talking in mid-sentence. It came in great waves, recreating for us the scene inside the theatre, the dancers on the stage, the flowers, the orchestra, the audience. And I remembered the tears on Anna de Lisle's cheeks at the end of *Swan Lake*.

'Here we go,' Hugo said softly as the applause finally died away.

He jammed on his head, at a rakish angle, a wide-brimmed black hat that he had been nursing in his lap. He started the engine. Simon, leaning over the seat in front, opened and held ajar the door on the right side of the car. There was nothing for me to do. We strained our eyes, watching.

After a hiatus of time the stage door opened, throwing a narrow band of light across the cobbles, and a sleek marmalade cat stepped fastidiously into the night. Baranov's note had said: 'Drive by stage door at once the cat leaves.' The cat had left. The Mercedes accelerated gently but steadily. We reached the stage door, slowed to a crawl, passed it, stopped. Nobody came out. There was no sign of Baranov or of anyone else.

Peering through the back window I could see the cat relieving itself by the wall of the theatre, and a few cars, a small van and a motor-bike, with a helmet attached to the handlebars, parked along the street. Everything looked dark and dank and slightly sinister. But this was because of the high, blank buildings. In fact, it was all very peaceful.

Nevertheless, we couldn't stay where we were, just beyond the stage door, with the engine running. We were inviting suspicion. Reluctantly Hugo backed the car until we were in our former position. We waited.

'We – ell,' Hugo said, 'St Michael and Ste Gudule seem to have taken us too literally. No scandal but no Baranov. Altogether a non-event. At least it doesn't seem to be a trap.'

'I suppose it couldn't be a sort of Russian joke?' Simon said tentatively. 'If they knew or guessed how Baranov had tried to defect they could have forced him to give that note to Lady Rayle just to make fools of us. The part about the cat still strikes me as very odd.'

'My dear boy, the KGB don't waste their energy,' Hugo said, dismissing the idea out of hand. 'I expect the only time that door's unlocked and possibly unguarded is when the cat is doing its business. Baranov's not a fool. Like most people, Simon, you think every Russian's either a spy or an ignorant peasant, whereas – '

'Look!' I interrupted them. 'Look!'

I pointed at the suddenly broadened band of light now streaming from the back of the theatre. A figure in mauve tights and purple doublet slid into the street and looked wildly from side to side before starting to run towards us. Hugo was accelerating. Simon had swung open the car door. Baranov leaped for the front seat and, helped by Simon, scrambled in. Simon, reaching over him, slammed and locked the door. The Mercedes had already begun to gather speed.

Behind us there were shouts and the sound of running feet. Then came the roar of a car engine, drowned by the more violent firing of a motor-bike. Simon and I were both looking out of the rear window. Baranov, twisting round in his seat, was more interested in me.

'Lady Rayle? It is Lady Rayle?'

'Yes. I'm Catherine Rayle. Are you all right?'

'Yes. I am fine now. You are Lady Rayle. I met you at the Belgian reception. I am Baranov. No mistakes this time.'

'For God's sake,' Hugo said, 'can't we leave the socializing for later? Simon, what's happening?'

'Two of them,' Simon said. 'A big black Ford and a motor-bike. They're not far behind. The bike may be a nuisance. It can tag us in traffic.'

'That is Igor Maniev in the car,' Baranov said. 'He watch me all the time. He won't leave my dressing-room. And I hit him to get away. I'm afraid Lady Rayle does not wait. The one on the – '

'Later,' Hugo said impatiently. 'Tell us later.'

'If you say,' Baranov said; he didn't like it – his nerves were taut and he felt a need to talk. We were through the Place de la Monnaie now and heading up the Rue Neuve to the Boulevard du Jardin Botanique. There was less traffic than one might have expected; most people going into the centre of the city to spend the evening had already arrived and it was still too early for more than a few to be leaving. But Hugo seemed to me to be driving in erratic bursts.

Simon kept up a running commentary on our pursuers. 'It's that bloody motor-cyclist,' he said. 'We might have made a break at the last lights but he's clinging to our tail. Igor, or whatever he calls himself, is following that yellow helmet of his. It's too easy for Comrade Igor.'

'Following could be the operative word,' Hugo said. 'Maybe they've settled for knowing who we are and where we're going.'

He pulled out, forestalling another car that hooted angrily, and we swept on to the ring-road. 'Let's tempt them on the boulevards and find out, shall we? If they want to try something, this is the place. If they're not to be tempted at least we'll know they don't intend immediate rescue.'

I took a deep breath. Being chased by purposeful Russians along the boulevards which caterpillar around the centre of Brussels, above and below ground, was not pleasant. Waiting for them 'to try something' that could result in an appalling accident was much worse, especially in the tunnels. We hurtled along, seeming because of the camber of the road to shave the walls, and the claustrophobic roof pressed the noise down on our heads. I sweated. Still the Russians did nothing. However fast, or slow, we went the motor-cyclist stayed just behind us as if on a towrope and, farther back, at a more elastic distance came the Ford.

I had begun to feel that we might go on like this for ever when, at last, the Russians decided to take some action.

The Ford, which was closer to us than it had been for some time, suddenly flicked its lights. The motor-cyclist, acknowledging the signal, drew out and began to overtake us. Simon shouted a warning but there was little that Hugo could do. Ahead of him two cars restricted his speed and he couldn't try to pass them because he was obstructed by the Russian. Instead, coming into a long, tight curve underground, he braked. Behind him the red rear warning lights of the Ford were reflected from the tunnel walls as it slowed correspondingly. The motor-cyclist's yellow helmet was now level with our car; he was turning his head to stare into the windows and I hunched my shoulder to make it as difficult as possible for him to get a clear view of Simon and myself. We were never to know if that was all he intended.

Without any warning Baranov leaned across Hugo and jerked open the door beside him. Hugo, startled, braked harder. The door swung back on its hinges. The motor-cyclist swerved, and the yellow helmet disappeared downwards out of my line of vision as he lost his balance. The Mercedes bumped sickeningly as a back wheel went over something. Hugo slowed to a crawl.

'God!' he said. 'Oh God! You bloody little savage! You've made me kill him!'

'On! On!' Baranov's voice was hoarse. 'He was a bad man. KGB. He – '

Simon interrupted him. 'Igor's not stopping. He's driven round the bike. He's coming after us. Go on, Hugo! You must!'

I leaned over Hugo's shoulder and, holding on to the back of his seat, managed to catch and shut the swinging door. I didn't really mean it as an encouragement to drive on. I wasn't thinking clearly. I had shut the door only because it was a danger, but it must have seemed like acquiescence. At any rate Hugo really didn't have much choice. Swearing horribly, he slammed his foot on the accelerator and we shot away.

We came off the boulevards at the next exit and wound our way through a maze of streets. Hugo drove hard but Igor, with luck on his side, managed to stay with us. Nobody spoke except Simon, who continuously reported the Ford's progress. Personally, I felt sick and I imagine Hugo and Simon did too. God knows what Baranov was thinking.

We were in a residential district now. I didn't know this part of Brussels but I had realized that we were more or less quartering the neighbourhood. There was one intersection with lights and a fair amount of traffic which we had been through twice. We were approaching it for the third time.

The lights were green. Hugo slowed. The cars ahead of us accelerated across the intersection. The lights went yellow and Hugo crawled towards them, preparing to stop. The Ford drew up behind us. Igor seized his chance.

'He's got a radiophone in the Ford,' Simon said, 'and he's using it. He could be reporting, demanding reinforcements. Or sticking the police on to us.'

The lights went red. Simultaneously the Mercedes surged forward into the on-coming traffic. There was a good deal of hooting and screeching of brakes and swearing but nobody hit us. Somehow we got across and Hugo hurled the car into a pretty, tree-lined street.

'Did the bastard make it?'

'No. You left him sitting.'

'But he'll have seen which way we went.' Hugo sounded pleased.

He turned right and right again. Then, unexpectedly, he stopped and reversed into an open garage, which appeared to be part of a small block of flats.

'Get out!' he said. 'Quick as you can.'

He was already running around the car to the front of the garage, slamming down the big door. I climbed by the front seat, followed by Simon. Baranov, incongruous and shivering in his ballet costume, got out the other side. Hugo, not taking his eyes from a small window set in the garage door, stripped off his raincoat. He threw it towards Baranov.

'Put that on!'

'Where are we?'

'Do as you're told.'

Simon had opened a door, which seemed to lead into a flat, but only enough to let a certain amount of light into the garage. 'Lock it after you,' he said to me. A couple of cars went by outside. Baranov was struggling into Hugo's raincoat, which was much too big for him. And a third car went by, slowly.

'There he is!' Hugo said. 'There's Igor and he's looking for us all right. He's reasoned that either he's lost us or we're trying to fox him. He's cruising around.' He started to swing up the garage door. 'Take Baranov into the kitchen, Kit. Wait for me there.'

Simon was already in the Mercedes, with the engine running. Hugo's big black hat was pulled well down over his fair hair. Simon, I realized, was going to act as a decoy to get Igor out of the neighbourhood. I didn't like the idea of that, not one bit. After what had happened to the motor-cyclist Igor would be in a murderous mood and Simon alone was very vulnerable. There was also a possibility that by now the police would be on the look-out for the Mercedes.

'Hurry, Kit!' Hugo said, and I went, taking Baranov.

From the kitchen window I saw Hugo standing in the road and beckoning urgently to Simon. The Mercedes roared out and away. Hugo ran back into the garage. I heard him shut the garage door before he came into the kitchen. He gave me a half grin.

'I need a drink,' he said.

'Simon –' I began.

'Not to worry,' he said. 'He'll be all right.'

I locked the door from the garage and left the key in the lock. Hugo went ahead through a small, square hall into a living-room pleasantly furnished with modern pieces and bright, original paintings. Busy finding a bottle of whisky and some glasses – he was very much at home – he answered my unspoken question.

'This flat belongs to a friend of mine, a girl named Lena. She's a singer at Le Domaine. Very good. It's worth going there to hear her.'

'What about the Mercedes? Does that belong to her too?'

'No. That's her boy-friend's.'

'Oh!'

'Kit! I said a friend of mine. I meant a friend. Originally Lena and her brother came from East Germany. I was – instrumental, shall we say, in getting them here. Which means she owes me.'

'I understand.'

'I doubt it. But no matter. The point is that Lena's prepared to do anything I ask. I can depend on her. What's more, her boy-friend's a pretty influential character in the Brussels administration. And that could be useful too.' He turned to Baranov. 'Whisky?'

Baranov waved away the glass that Hugo was offering him. '*Niet*,' he said. 'I do not drink that. I do not like it. And I do not like this house. I think it does not have diplomatic – safety. So why do you bring me here? Is Sergei here? If not –'

'If not, you'll go running back to your Russian chums like last time?' Hugo asked.

'I do not understand. I have not –'

'Now, look, I've had a gutsful of –'

'Hugo! Monsieur Baranov is my – my guest.' I didn't like him any more than Hugo did but that was irrelevant. 'How long do we have to stay here, Hugo?'

'We can go whenever you like.'

'Good. Monsieur Baranov, we'll answer any questions we can when we get to the Residence.'

'And we'll have some to ask,' Hugo said.

We left by a back door which gave on to a garden, Hugo, Baranov and myself, in that order. It was dark – our only light was Hugo's pencil torch – and spitting with rain again. I thought longingly of Simon's umbrella, abandoned in the MG, but boots would have been more use. The garden didn't seem to have a path and we waded through thick, wet grass, past some dustbins and out into a muddy lane. Once Baranov slipped, nearly fell, and let flow a spate of Russian. Once a dog barked very close to us and then followed us along the other side of a fence, sniffing at us. We saw nobody. But we were fully prepared to jump at shadows. It was an enormous relief to reach the end of the lane and Hugo's car.

Hugo owned both an Austin Princess, as befitted his ministerial rank, and a Rover. Usually he drove the Rover and left the Austin for Daphne. Tonight he had brought the big car. He bundled Baranov into the back, making him lie across my feet, and covered him with the lap rug. He threw me a chiffon scarf to disguise my hair. It was Daphne's; I recognized the scent she always used. And he put on a chauffeur's cap, which was somewhat too small for him. We now presented an imposing, diplomatic picture.

'You seem to have thought of everything,' I said, half resentfully.

'I did my best,' he said and added in rapid French, 'Notwithstanding, I've a nasty feeling it's not going to be good enough. The sooner this maniac's on his way to Israel, the happier I'll be.'

I couldn't disagree. I should be glad too when Baranov had gone. On the other hand I saw no reason at the moment for pessimism. We had collected the parcel safely. And the journey back to the Residence was being encouragingly uneventful; Hugo drove at a steady, relaxed chauffeur's pace and we saw no sign of Igor's Ford, which presumably was pursuing Simon. My spirits lifted as we turned into the drive and the house came into sight. The Residence had never looked more welcoming.

Chapter 7

I joined Hugo in the drawing-room. His appearance was extraordinary. From the waist up, Savile Row wouldn't have been ashamed of him. But, on his lower half, he was wearing a pair of too-tight trousers, bright yellow socks and suede slippers, all of which must have belonged to Simon; I had left him foraging for dry clothes in Simon's room while I took Baranov along to the suite that had been prepared for him. Hugo was on the telephone.

'My dear Lena, you're wonderful! I don't know what I'd have done without you.' He listened, laughed, said: *'A bientôt, chérie!'* and hung up.

He raised his glass, about a quarter full of neat whisky, in my direction. His face was grey and rather haggard. 'Well, that's dealt with the Mercedes.' He sighed, no longer pretending to be happy. 'On Monday, when her boy-friend returns from the weekend with his wife's family, Lena will tell him the car was stolen. He'll report it to the police, who'll understand that he lent it to a *petite amie* so that it wouldn't be wise to press their enquiries. And, if there's any fuss about the KGB man, they'll block the Russians. Oh God!' He gulped most of the whisky. 'Why did Baranov have to open that car door? He must have known what would happen.'

'He was afraid,' I said. 'Hugo – ' I wanted to ask him more about Lena's boy-friend, but there were immediate problems. 'I think there's trouble.'

'What sort of trouble?' He was impatient.

'Complications. Baranov says he won't co-operate unless – '

'Tell him to go to hell! After all we've done to save him from the KGB and – '

'That's just it.'

'What do you mean?'

'He says we've done nothing for him, nothing he couldn't have done for himself. He says he could have defected easily, whenever the Bolshoi came to the West, if he had set his mind to it - that he is Baranov and any country would be proud to give him asylum, that –'

'Stuff Baranov! If it was so easy for him why didn't he just up and do it then, instead of being such a bloody nuisance?'

'He – he says it was part of the bargain he made with the British. He was to defect in Brussels, to the NATO Ambassador – on condition that at the same time they would get Marika somebody or other out of East Germany. He wants to know where Marika is and what message she has sent him. He says he trusted the British.'

I stopped. My throat was dry. I went across to the butler's tray and helped myself to a small whisky and a lot of soda. I had been touched by Baranov's emotional outburst; he had wept when he spoke of his beautiful Jewess, Marika. Nevertheless, some of the implications of what he had said were dismaying. And it was dismay that I saw mirrored in Hugo's face.

'No, it wasn't the British Baranov trusted,' he said at last, emphasizing each word. 'It was that goddam character General Sir Richard Tindle, the last man – or woman – anyone should trust. And, as usual, Tindle expects someone else to clear up the mess he's made.' Hugo's voice shook with frustrated anger.

'We don't know – ' I began.

'Oh, don't we?' Hugo said. 'What more did Baranov have to say?'

'Not very much,' I said, and tried to explain.

In fact, he had said a great deal, but I hadn't understood half of it. His English was good, but accented, and the more excited he got at the idea that his Marika might not have escaped safely to the West, the more unintelligible he had become, interlarding his sentences with rapid Russian. None the less, I had got the gist of the story – or thought I had.

Baranov had met Marika about two years ago, when they were both guests at the *dacha* of one of the Party leaders. Baranov was there because he was Baranov. Marika had come with her boss, who was a VIP indeed, being the co-ordinator of arms production for the Soviet Union and its satellites. She was, as far as I could make out, some sort of personal assistant. She always travelled with him in the Soviet bloc, though never in the West, acted as his interpreter and was generally invaluable; as a result she was privy to a considerable amount of secret information.

Marika was a good communist but she was also a Jewess and she could not believe there was much of a future for anyone of her race in Russia. She and Baranov, who had discovered a thread of Jewish blood in his own veins, had determined to emigrate to Israel. The problem was how, since clearly neither of them would get permission. But, eventually, the problem seemed to solve itself. Their big chance came when Marika found that she would be visiting East Germany at the same time as Baranov was dancing in Brussels.

'At which point Dick and his friends botched it,' Hugo said viciously. 'At least we know why it was in Brussels that Baranov had to defect. Timing must have been of the essence if they were to get Marika out. I suppose Tindle's hoping to pick her brains. She must have lots of useful stuff.'

'Do you mean that Baranov's only – incidental?'

'I shouldn't be surprised. I'm not saying that Tindle isn't interested in ballet. He's got some unsuspected depths. But it could be he considers Baranov has no more than propaganda value. The girl, on the other hand, sounds as if she might be very important indeed to him.'

I sipped my soda and whisky and considered this new theory. I wished that Baranov had been more articulate. But his explanations had been confused by anger at what had already gone wrong and fear at what might yet go wrong, for Marika and Sergei . . .

I said: 'Hugo, there's somebody called Sergei Alexandrov who's connected with this, too.'

'Sergei! Yes, I remember,' Hugo said. 'He mentioned him when we were at Lena's flat. How the hell does Sergei fit in?'

'I don't know,' I said. 'I'm not even sure who Sergei is. Baranov's English got wilder and wilder. But something terrible seems to have happened to him.'

'Maybe he's the KGB chap I killed this evening,' Hugo said bitterly.

'No,' I said. 'Baranov seemed to think he might be here, in the Residence. I really didn't understand.'

'Oh Lord!' Hugo groaned. 'What did you say to all this?'

'I tried to calm him down. I told him I'd have news of Marika, and Sergei, tomorrow – surely Dick Tindle must know about them. And I suggested he get out of his muddy costume, have a hot bath and put on pyjamas and a dressing-gown. Incidentally, nobody thought of providing any clothes for him.'

'Well, nobody knew he was going to turn up dressed as Albrecht, did they?'

'I said I'd bring him up some supper in half an hour. I asked the servants to leave a tray for me as I had eaten early and didn't know when I'd be back. It'll be in the dining-room. But I had better try to telephone Dick first.'

'No! Don't do that, Kit.'

'Why not?'

'Because, before you do, there are one or two questions I'd like to put to Baranov – such as how he came to return to his Russian chums after Dick Tindle's people had got hold of him. The rest of it makes some sense, but that really sticks in my craw.'

It was the first thing Hugo asked when we got upstairs, and he phrased it badly. Baranov, who had been looking with interest at the chicken salad and fruit that I had brought him, waited for Hugo to pour some champagne.

'It is simple,' he said coldly. 'I did not leave your friends. I was never with them. You make mistakes always. I tell you.' He began to eat, very quickly. 'It was Sergei Alexandrov your friends took the other night. They took him instead of me. When the cars collided Sergei was thrown against the door frame and was not conscious. He crumpled on the floor. I tried to pick him up, and also I unlocked the car door. A thin man with a long, pale face flung it open and started to pull Sergei out on to the road. I clung to Sergei. Igor clung to me.'

Baranov paused for a moment and I caught Hugo's eye. He

was clearly as appalled by what we had just heard as I was. Baranov drank some champagne, then went on.

'A great giant of a man came to Igor's side of the car where the door had burst open. He seized Igor and me, one in each hand, and threw us together in a heap. Everything was very confused. A third man came with his face all covered in blood. They started to carry Sergei away and our driver – the one who tonight was killed on the motor-cycle – shoots at them. They run for safety. Sergei just stands. He is dazed. Igor shouts to him to come back to us and to the driver to shoot no more, but he shoots just the same and – and – Sergei is hit.'

Baranov gulped. I thought he was going to cry again but he managed to control himself. 'Poor Sergei! He was my friend. He helped me. Yes. But he does not want to leave Russia or the Bolshoi. It was bad and foolish to shoot him. So, I am not sorry I made that accident in the tunnel.'

'An eye for an eye,' Hugo murmured, 'and the reciprocal tooth.'

Baranov looked at him blankly; his Jewishness did not yet extend to the Old Testament. He said: 'I wanted to go to help Sergei but Igor wouldn't let me. He was afraid for me. And the man with the bloody face returned and made the big man pick up Sergei and they carried him to their car and drove away. Igor said we must go, quickly, before the police come, so we went. But you – do you yet know what has happened to Sergei?'

'He's being cared for,' I said. 'Luckily his wound isn't serious. He will be well soon.' I hoped that I was telling him the truth.

'Good! Good!' he said. 'If only tomorrow you have such news of Marika I will do whatever you wish. I am so glad about Sergei. Perhaps he will now come with us to Israel and he and I will dance together again.'

'There is just one thing,' Hugo said. 'I can understand that even after the disaster on Tuesday night you still wanted to defect, but – '

'No, I am not defecting!' Baranov said. 'I am emigrating – to Israel. And I shall continue to love Russia even though I am leaving her.'

'All right!' Hugo said. 'I'll call you an emigrant, if you like.

But the KGB will call you a traitor, and if they have the faintest idea that you're at this Residence –' He left the sentence unfinished.

'How could they know where I am?'

'Didn't they question you after Sergei was carried off like that? He was your friend, you say.'

'Yes. They questioned me all night and most of the next day so that I cannot dance. But they say I must dance and it is dreadful. I have never danced as badly, never.' He shook his head sadly. 'And I told them nothing they did not know already. Igor himself saw everything that happened. As for Sergei, what was there to tell them about him?'

'You didn't tell them the men who had taken Sergei were British?'

'No!'

'Igor knew this?'

'No! How could he? They did not look British. They did not speak British. They spoke French. I do not think they themselves were British. Perhaps the one with the bloody face.'

'At any rate, the British arranged it. You knew that. But how did you know that it was Lady Rayle you were meant to come to?'

If Hugo expected Baranov to be nonplussed by this question he was disappointed. Baranov, who had been getting a little irritated by Hugo's inquisition, looked pleased with himself.

'I know, as you say, that the British are to arrange everything and that, somehow, NATO is concerned. Staying in my Embassy, it is easy. I look up the diplomatic list for the British Ambassador to NATO. And I decide, if Lady Rayle comes to the Belgian reception, to risk everything. Even so I nearly missed recognizing her because a stupid girl tries to kiss me. Still, all is well now, if only Marika –'

'We'll let you know tomorrow,' Hugo said and stood up abruptly. He seemed to have run out of questions. 'Good night.'

'Monsieur Baranov,' I said, 'I hope you'll be able to sleep. And I hope you'll soon be with Marika again.'

'Thank you,' he said.

I gave him some instructions about keeping his door locked

and being as quiet as possible, and we went downstairs. I felt very sorry for him. Beneath his arrogance and egotism he was an extremely frightened young man – the future, even with Marika, must have looked terrifyingly unknown – but he was also a mercurial character. I didn't think he was going to be an easy guest.

Hugo was again on the telephone when I reached the drawing-room. He was listening intently. Suddenly he banged down the receiver.

'Just breathing,' he said. 'Do you get many calls like that, Kit?'

'I don't think so,' I said, 'but I don't usually answer the phone myself, not unless I'm expecting someone to ring or I know the houseman's out.'

'No, of course not. I shouldn't have answered it either. Sorry. I thought it might be Simon.'

'It's not important.' I hoped it hadn't been Daphne checking up on Hugo's whereabouts. 'Probably a wrong number. Do you want to wait while I try to telephone Dick Tindle?'

'I suggest you leave that till morning. Go into the office and use the secure line, then you can say what you want. And remember, as far as you're concerned there are two things that are essential. To find out about Marika so as to keep Baranov happy, and to impress on Tindle that you want Baranov out of the Residence as soon as possible.'

'All right. That sounds reasonable.'

'It is reasonable. And, Kit.'

'Yes?'

'Don't let Tindle persuade you to do anything more. It's up to him to deal with Baranov and Sergei and the rest. Tell him from me that you can't cope by yourself and that I positively refuse to help any more.'

'And do you?'

'Yes, I do. First thing tomorrow morning I'm off to Paris. I promised Daphne and I refuse to disappoint her. Why should I?' Hugo smiled at me. 'I'll be back on Monday. And by then, with any luck, your famous house guest will have departed. I'm sorry, Kit, but that's the way it has to be. Incidentally, don't cancel any of your engagements this weekend. If anybody has to mind the shop, let it be Simon. The last thing you want while Baranov's here is to draw attention to yourself.'

The sound of Simon's MG roaring up the drive stilled the tart reply that was hovering on my tongue. Common sense told me that Hugo was right, but all the same I felt let down. During the week I received too many invitations, official, semi-official and unofficial, but weekends were different. People seemed to reserve them for their families and getting out of Brussels and such socializing as there was didn't reach to an ambassadorial level. Indeed I often went from Friday night to Monday morning without speaking to anyone except the servants. To be told not to cancel any of my engagements, therefore, was griping, especially when Hugo and Daphne were going off to enjoy themselves in Paris. And Simon, I thought, had done enough.

He came in now, looking complacent because everything had gone well. He had picked Igor up quickly – as expected, Igor had been combing the streets for some sign of our car – and led him once more around Brussels before tricking him by abandoning the Mercedes and running through the arcade to the Rue de Persil. He had then driven back past the Mercedes in his MG, and had actually seen Igor examining the deserted car. In fact, the contingency plan had worked perfectly. Simon grinned at us.

'To tell the truth,' he said, 'I've rather enjoyed this evening. I'm sorry the excitement's all over.'

The next morning, after a brief visit to Baranov, who seemed reasonably content, I set off for the office. I was there by nine-thirty; any earlier on a Saturday would have been extraordinary. Immediately I dialled Dick Tindle's London number. I expected an acrimonious argument about whether or not he was available and sighed when I recognized the sharp, clipped tones of his deputy. I was determined to talk only to Dick. But I didn't get a chance.

'Good morning, Lady Rayle. I've been waiting for your telephone call.' The voice was as incisive as ever but less acid; I had never met its owner. 'Let me say at once that it is impossible to speak to Sir Richard. He is not, at present, in the United Kingdom. However, he has instructed me to relay certain information to you. But first I must ask if the parcel has arrived safely?'

'Yes,' I said. 'It's at the Residence.'

'And in good condition?' he persisted.

'For God's sake,' I said. 'I thought this was meant to be a secure line. If you mean Baranov, yes, he's in good condition, at least physically, but he's worried about his – '

'Lady Rayle,' he interrupted me. 'That's excellent news. However, even on secure voice, you know, it may be wiser to avoid well-known names.' He paused for my comment but I held my tongue and he continued. 'Now, let me give you Sir Richard's message. It's a trifle complicated, I'm afraid. He says: Tell B that Marika is also safe and well and sends her love. And "Love, love – tradition tells us – is the joining of a soul with a kindred soul, their union, their conjunction . . ." Have you got that? Would you repeat it, please?'

I repeated it and he thanked me. He even explained that it was a line from one of Fyedor Tyutchev's poems, that it should satisfy B completely and that there was no reason now why the next phase should not commence at once. I assumed he meant the arrangements for Baranov to leave the Residence.

'Good!' I had achieved Hugo's two essentials – news of Marika and assurance that Baranov would soon be on his way. Until I could speak to Dick I saw no point in explaining what had happened last night but thought I should mention Sergei. 'Just one other thing,' I said. 'On Tuesday your people in Brussels made something of a hash of things.'

'Yes,' he said, 'that was unfortunate. Sir Richard was far from pleased when we were informed that there would be a delay. However, all's well now, isn't it?'

'Yes,' I said. 'Everything's fine, except for Sergei Alexandrov.'

'Sergei Alexandrov?'

'The other dancer your people took on Tuesday. Presumably he's still with them. He's B's friend and B wants to know what's happening to him. He says Sergei was prepared to help, but he didn't want to defect himself. What shall I tell B?'

'Tell him – tell him that Sergei is safe and well – like Marika.'

'And is he?'

'Lady Rayle, I haven't the faintest idea. But I propose to find out. Meanwhile I imagine you'll be getting hold of the Secretary General and – '

'The Secretary General!'

'What else would you suggest? We've kept our side of the bargain. It's up to B to keep his.' His voice sharpened suddenly. 'Lady Rayle, hasn't B told you that Marika entrusted him with invaluable intelligence which he is to give to the West?'

'No, he hasn't. This is the first I've heard of any "invaluable intelligence". So far B has talked almost exclusively about himself and Marika and Sergei.'

'I see.' There was a pause. 'That's very interesting. He could be waiting until he's sure Marika is safe, of course, or alternatively . . . Yes, we'll have to consider that possibility.'

I let him consider his possibility. I had a problem of my own. The casual reference to the Secretary General had surprised me. It still did. Obviously the British had helped Marika to escape from behind the Iron Curtain and had planned Baranov's simultaneous defection in return for some promise of information. Why, having acquired it, they were then preparing to hand over the information, presumably sight unseen, to NATO was incomprehensible, at any rate to me. Surely no country was as altruistic as all that. No diplomat worth his salt would put NATO before his own –

'You expect me to take Baranov to the Secretary General?' I said. 'Out of the blue? What do you suppose one of your career diplomats would do with a suggestion like that? Tell me! Anyway, he's away till Wednesday.'

'Lady Rayle, this is no time to quibble about – '

But I was determined to make him spell it out. 'I can easily ask Hugo Pewter, or even Sir Thomas Bright.'

'Well, he would – would consult with London first.'

'With your crowd?' I didn't bother to hide my feelings.

'He would refer the matter to his immediate superior.'

'Thank you. Yes, that's rather what I thought.'

At last the pieces were beginning to fit together. At last I understood why I, or someone like me, had been essential to Dick Tindle's schemes. Given 'invaluable intelligence', only the

Lady Amateur who, as everyone knew, had a bee in her bonnet about NATO's role, would go dashing off to the Secretary General before consulting her own Foreign Office. The Jeanne d'Arc act that Dick had encouraged hadn't been a lot of guff as Hugo had suggested; it had been intended to set the scene for my producing Baranov before the NATO Council. Why Dick wanted me to do this was still a mystery, but want it he did – and he'd thought me fool enough to play my part without question. I tasted gall.

Chapter 8

It's difficult to have a row on the long-distance telephone with someone you've never met who continues to be icily polite whatever you say. But I did my best.

Dick Tindle's deputy, having decided that I wasn't reacting as expected of Jeanne d'Arc, had proceeded to give me orders – and I mean orders; he had none of Dick's charm or powers of persuasion. I was to arrange an appointment with the Secretary General immediately he returned to Brussels, confront him with Baranov and demand that Baranov be given a hearing by the Council. When I protested that things simply didn't work that way at NATO he told me that it was up to me to be sure that on this occasion they did. He also gave me a lot of extraordinary instructions about Baranov, who, he feared, might no longer be trustworthy once the Bolshoi had gone home.

The bloody man! He had put me in a foul mood. As Rule drove out of the gate into the service road I looked back through the rear window of the Rolls at the ugly squat NATO buildings – at best they are a depressing sight – and swore that I would never go near them again. I would go back to the Residence and write out my resignation. Dick Tindle could . . .

Of course I didn't mean it. I have far too much sense of responsibility. And, I reminded myself, though I might be Catherine Rayle – historian, scholar, author – and not just some silly little bitch, in Dick's world I was a babe in arms; my intelligence functioned on a different level. Besides, I had gone too far to back out. I would have to see the job through, however unpalatable it was.

We were bowling up the drive by this time, and my temper had cooled. I went straight upstairs to see Baranov. To my surprise he was deep in a game of chess with Simon. And he was winning. Simon was none too pleased about it; he continued to study the board while I lied to Baranov about Sergei and gave him Marika's message.

When I quoted the lines from Fyedor Tyutchev, Baranov went mad. He clapped his hands, shouted with joy and, kicking off his slippers, performed a *pas seul.* The floor shook. The chessboard went flying. A chair was knocked over. I seized a vase of flowers just in time and, remembering the servants, made Baranov stop.

'I'm so happy,' he said, 'so happy. I bless you, Lady Rayle! I bless Simon too and Comrade Hugo. I bless all the British.'

I saw the broad grin on Simon's face as he anticipated Hugo's reaction to comradeship. Then he caught my eye and the grin faded. My expression must have been bleak. Mindful of what Dick's deputy had said, I was wondering how long Baranov's gratitude would last.

'Unfortunately, Monsieur Baranov, the rest of the news isn't as good,' I said. 'The Secretary General is at present in Norway, which means you'll not be able to give him the important information you have brought us until next Wednesday, or even possibly Thursday.'

'I cannot wait for Wednesday,' Baranov said simply. He lay flat on his back on the carpet and began to do limbering-up exercises. 'Already I get stiff. It is nice here in these rooms but there is no *barre* and no space to practise. A dancer must dance every day.'

'I'm sorry,' I said. 'If you had come on Tuesday – '

'And whose fault that I do not come on Tuesday?' Baranov had leapt to his feet in one fluid movement and stood facing me. In the jeans and T-shirt Simon had bought him he looked very young; he also looked supremely sure of himself. 'I stay – for Monday. If your General does not arrive I see his deputy. It is the same thing.'

'No, I'm afraid not,' I said. 'The deputy doesn't carry enough weight with the Council. It must be the Secretary General.'

Behind Baranov's back Simon was frowning and shaking his head at me. He didn't know what we were talking about, but the idea of Baranov giving important information direct to the

Secretary General appalled him; he was sure the Office hadn't been consulted. I ignored him. I watched Baranov as that sharp, clipped voice from London had told me to do.

'Very well,' Baranov shrugged. 'I see who you like, Lady Rayle. I tell him what I am instructed. Because you keep your side of the bargain, I keep mine.' His sudden change of attitude wasn't very convincing, but his wide mouth had widened into a smile. 'As for now, I think only of my Marika,' he said firmly.

'Quite right,' Simon said. 'We should drink to Marika and your reunion with her.'

'Yes, yes!' Baranov said, applauding. 'Let us have champagne.'

We spent the next fifteen minutes talking about Israel; none of us had ever been there. Simon promised to lend Baranov a novel set in Jerusalem and I said I would look out one or two histories for him. Baranov asked if we had any books on Brussels; he always liked to read about cities he had visited.

'I'll bring you a couple of guide books,' I said. 'But now we must go. We'll arrange some lunch for you shortly, Monsieur Baranov.'

'Do not forget the costume,' he said to Simon as we got up.

'What costume?'

Simon looked embarrassed. 'Is it all right, Lady Rayle? Baranov said I might have the clothes he wore as Albrecht in exchange for the gear I bought him this morning.'

'Why not?' I was surprised he had thought it necessary to ask me.

'Thank you,' he said. 'And thank you, Baranov, very much. I'll – I'll be back.'

Outside the door, his arms full of purple and silver mud-stained, tawdry garments, Simon hesitated. 'Lady Rayle, I know it's not up to me to advise you, but – '

'That's so,' I said incisively. 'It is not up to you to advise me, Simon, unless of course I ask you for advice. On this particular occasion I don't want it. I have already decided not to send the appropriate telegrams to the Office but to take Baranov direct to the Secretary General. You'll have to take my word for it – this is important for NATO, for the Western Alliance, not just for the UK.'

'But at least he should be vetted first, Lady Rayle. He – he could be a Russian plant.'

'Baranov – an agent? Don't be silly.' I laughed. 'Go and put that stuff of his away, Simon – somewhere the servants won't come on it – then get the great man his lunch. He'll have to make do with some of the exotic tins Anna de Lisle bought. Tell him we'll try to do better for dinner.'

'Yes – all right, Lady Rayle.'

Simon gave me a long, hard look. I could see him counting the hours till Monday afternoon, when Hugo would be back from Paris and he could tell him that the events of the past week had finally driven me round the bend.

The weekend wasted uneventfully away. On Sunday evening I worked until after midnight on the definitive book about NATO that I hoped some day to publish. Then I made myself some black coffee and went upstairs. I didn't undress. I pulled up a chair by the window so that I could look out on the garden. It was a crisp, clear night with a horned moon, a good night for what I had been told to expect. I read by the light of a small table lamp.

About three o'clock my head was nodding. The bed looked very inviting. It was a temptation to believe that Dick Tindle's deputy had been wrong but I couldn't risk it. If I woke up and found that Baranov was missing I would never forgive myself.

I walked up and down the room. I did some simple exercises. And the electric tea-maker that I keep beside my bed made me a cup of tea which helped more than anything.

At four-thirty there was a slight, scuffling sound in the corridor. Somebody had fallen over the chair I had moved from its usual position against the wall. I flung open my door, letting the light stream out. Nobody was in sight. He would, I thought, move like a cat and I had been slow. I ran down the corridor, through Simon's sitting-room and into his bedroom, switching on more lights as I went.

Dick Tindle's deputy had not been wrong.

'What the hell's going on?'

Simon, wakened by the sudden light, was sitting up in bed.

He stared from me to Baranov and back again. Baranov was standing at the head of the stairs that led down to the conservatory, his hand still on the door-knob. Yesterday afternoon, when the houseman and the cook had gone off to visit relations in Malines, I had taken Baranov down those stairs and into the grounds for some air and exercise; and he had shown almost as much interest in the layout of the place as had Anna de Lisle the previous weekend. He had also been enthralled by the guide books on Brussels and the English newspapers I had provided for him. The Sundays had all carried headlines about the Bolshoi's misfortunes in the Belgian capital, two of their great dancers – Baranov and Sergei Alexandrov – taken ill, and another member of their party killed by a hit-and-run driver; inevitably the Company had cut short their tour; they were flying home that day. And Baranov had decided that it was now time for him to leave the Residence.

'What the hell's going on?' Simon repeated.

I said nothing. I looked at Baranov, waiting to hear what he would say.

'I'm sorry,' he said. 'I was not feeling well so I came to find Simon. I did not mean to disturb anybody.'

'Which is why you didn't knock on Simon's door or switch on the light?' I said. 'Fair enough. But why, Monsieur Baranov, are you dressed and carrying your shoes?'

He glowered at me. 'You know, Lady Rayle. Why ask me?'

'I wish I did,' Simon said. 'Won't someone explain?'

'Monsieur Baranov was about to leave us,' I said. 'He thinks we have served our purpose. He feels safe since the Bolshoi have gone home and he never intended, if it could be avoided, to provide the Secretary General with any information that might harm the USSR. He is not a traitor. He doesn't even like to be called a defector. He wants to emigrate to Israel with Marika – and a clear conscience. Isn't that so, Monsieur Baranov?'

'You cannot stop me. Marika said –'

'Yes. Go on. We know it was Marika who planned everything, Monsieur Baranov. We didn't think it was you. She's a clever girl.'

'You cannot stop me,' he said again. 'You cannot keep me here against my will.'

'I wouldn't dream of trying,' I said cheerfully. 'You may leave whenever you like. Presumably you won't want to arrive at the Israeli Embassy in my official car – or are you going to the Americans? But I'm sure Simon will drive you.'

'Now?' Simon said. He had slid out of bed and put on dressing-gown and slippers. 'I doubt if they'll let us into the Israeli Chancery at this time of the morning. Or do you mean we should go to the Ambassador's Residence?'

'Whatever Monsieur Baranov wants,' I said. 'However –'

Baranov had been expecting some proviso – he was far from being a fool – and his little pointed chin came up to take the blow. He was sure it would be only a temporary setback. After all, Marika was safe in England and I couldn't hope to keep him at the Residence for very long without his co-operation. His primary embarrassment at having been caught sneaking away was forgotten. Beneath his self-confidence his arrogance showed. It never occurred to him that the stupid Brits might have outwitted his clever Marika. So the chop, when I made it, was the more devastating.

'Monsieur Baranov,' I said. 'The British have kept their side of the bargain. In spite of your KGB you are here in a safe house. Marika, now in the West, is also safe. However, we foresaw that, once you had brought this about, you might be a little reluctant to do your part. So we took precautions. As I said, Marika is safe – but she is still in West Berlin, and the parcel we brought out from East Berlin could just as easily be returned.'

There was a breath-holding silence. Simon and Baranov both stared at me in amazement, Simon because such ruthlessness was a new and unbelievable facet of my character and Baranov because he could not accept that Marika's plan had come unstuck.

'No!' he said. 'No! You lie. The poetry. The lines from Fyedor Tyutchev. It – it was to make sure . . .' He finished in a flood of Russian.

'Yes,' I said. 'You arranged with Marika that she would send you those lines from a love poem as a message only if she was already in England. But she was tricked.' I hoped he wouldn't ask me; I had no idea how Dick Tindle had tricked her. 'At the moment she is perfectly safe, but close to the border with East Berlin. And she will stay there till you've done what you undertook to do. Of course, if you choose to go to the Israelis or the Americans we shan't try to stop you, but I shall make a telephone call and the parcel will be moved immediately. The choice is yours, Monsieur Baranov.'

'*Niet. Niet.* Marika . . .' Murmuring Russian that sounded like a lament but could have been a curse on me and all the British, Baranov sank to the ground. His body seemed to wilt. Forgetting that the Russians had ordained that *Swan Lake* should have a happy ending, I saw him as the traditional dying Siegfried, his Odette lost for ever. And, in spite of the raincoat, the jeans, the T-shirt, he was a moving figure, not least because he was unaware that he was acting. Deliberately I ignored his histrionics.

'Don't worry too much, Monsieur Baranov,' I said. 'I'm sure everything will have sorted itself out by the end of the week.'

Somehow it didn't sound as reassuring as I had intended.

After all that it was a very short night and, though I had managed about three hours' sleep, I was not feeling my best to face Monday. So, until it was time to go to Brussels International to welcome the Deputy Chief of the Defence Staff who was flying in from London, I decided to work at home. I was sitting at my desk, trying to prepare a speech for the Atlantic Assembly, when Simon, who was to go to the airport with me, came in. He was clearly upset.

'What's the matter?'

'I can't do anything with Baranov. He refuses to have any breakfast. He refuses to get up or wash or dress. He's lying on his bed in those beautiful silk pyjamas Anna bought him, getting tight on champagne and saying that he'll never dance again.'

'What a wonderful picture.' I laughed – and saw Simon's face. 'Oh, for God's sake, don't look so reproachful, Simon! I'm not hard-hearted. Baranov's a great dancer, but that doesn't make him a great man. And at the moment he's half acting, half sulking and half being sorry for himself.'

'Yes, Lady Rayle. I'm sure you're right,' Simon said ruefully.

'Even though you've divided him into three halves. But about his girl-friend, Marika – our people wouldn't really return her to the communists, would they?'

'I doubt it. They expect her to be very useful to them.'

'Good! I'm glad. Poor old Baranov! I can't help feeling sorry for him and his Marika.'

'Well, don't be too sorry for them,' I said hastily, 'because if you as much as give him a hint that Marika's in no danger he'll walk out on us. Then it's yourself and Polly you'll need to be sorry for.'

'What – what do you mean?'

'I mean it'll be the end of your otherwise promising career, Simon. And Sir Thomas Bright isn't going to let his only child marry a failed diplomat.'

'Damn!' Simon said. 'It was supposed to be a secret – I mean about Polly and me. Her old man doesn't know yet. Hugo told you?'

'In fact, it was Daphne. She seemed to think I'd appreciate the comparison with herself and Hugo – marrying the ambassador's daughter and all that.'

'Really? Well, Polly wouldn't appreciate it,' he said shortly. 'She's no schoolgirl bride and, if I've got anything to do with it, she's not going to be a spoilt, childless wife either.'

'Simon!'

'I – I'm sorry, Lady Rayle.'

'So you should be,' I said. I tried not to smile. 'No matter. The important thing is not to forget what I said about Baranov. Do you – '

There was a rap on the door. The houseman came in. He was an efficient, French-speaking Belgian, who had served a succession of British ambassadors in Brussels. His wife was part Flemish. They both seemed trustworthy and discreet.

He said in French: 'Your Excellency, I'm sorry to trouble you but the maintenance men have come to inspect the Residence.'

'Again? Surely it's no time since it was inspected?'

He shrugged his incomprehension at the lavish way governments maintained their properties abroad. 'I told them to start upstairs. Later they'll want to look at this room, if you don't mind.'

'No. I shall be leaving soon.' But I didn't want them wandering around, not with Baranov here.

'Upstairs,' Simon said, laying peculiar emphasis on the word.

'Yes,' I said. 'You go.' And to the houseman: 'Where are the men now?'

'One of them went to the van to fetch something, I think. The other went straight upstairs. Is – is something wrong, Your Excellency?'

'No, I don't suppose so. But nobody told us to expect them today. Are they the same men who came last time?'

'Not the same, no. I've not seen this couple before. They said they were new. And, of course, it's a very large firm. They maintain a lot of foreign property in Brussels, not only the British.'

'Yes.' I stood up. In spite of the warmth of the room I felt cold. I was probably panicking for no reason. But these men, who seemed to have turned up out of the blue for an unnecessary inspection of the Residence, could be from – anywhere. 'I should like you to telephone their office and check,' I said. 'They may have made a mistake and come to the wrong Residence. Do that at once, will you, and let me know?'

'Very good, Your Excellency.'

As soon as the houseman left I hurried into the hall, seized a coat from the cloakroom and went out on to the drive. I had seen the workmen's van from the window. It had not been taken to the back of the house but had been driven around the long, oval-shaped flower-bed that lay in front of the main entrance, and parked at the top of the drive facing down the hill. It was a plain navy-blue van with no name and no windows in the back. Feeling rather silly, I memorized the number on the licence plate.

And almost immediately forgot it. As I walked to the front of the van to see if there was anyone in the driver's seat the head of a large Alsatian thrust itself out of the window, bared its teeth and growled deep in its throat. I like dogs. I like Alsatians; Guy had a beauty when we were first married so I know something about them, enough to recognize a true threat. This one was nobody's pet; this was a guard dog. And if I were rash enough to try to pat him I might well lose a finger. I didn't risk it. I went back to the house at a smart trot. There was nothing to be learnt from the van.

In the upstairs corridor I heard raised voices. Simon, speaking in fast but precise English, was sounding his most imperious.

'Why were you looking through the keyhole?'

'The door is locked.'

'Yes. It is my private office. It is always locked because I keep confidential papers there.'

'I must go in. Look in every place. Make *très bon*.'

'Show me your work order.'

'I don't understand.'

'Your order to inspect the British Residence. No order, no inspection.'

'We see.'

'Like hell we do! I don't believe you come from our maintenance firm at all. I think you're some sort of thief.'

'Your Excellency!' the houseman called to me from the bottom of the stairs.

'Oh!' Simon doubled up in sudden agony. The short, square man in blue overalls with whom he had been arguing had, without warning, punched him in the gut. Head down, the man now charged along the corridor. Brushing aside my minimal efforts to stop him, he started down the stairs. The houseman leaned backwards over the curving banister as if to avoid contact but, at the last moment, shot out his foot. The man had no chance. He seemed to dive in a long, flat movement, ending in a belly flop on the hall floor. At the same time he let forth a great roar of pain and anger.

He must have hurt himself considerably. If he had landed on the original parquet he might have been killed but the last ambassador had had the hall close-carpeted so that his fall was somewhat cushioned. Nevertheless, I would have expected him to have been winded but, almost at once, he was on his feet and running back to the servants' quarters.

Our reactions were slow. Simon was temporarily incapacitated, the houseman made no attempt to follow, and I reached the bottom of the stairs too late to take any effective action. Cook told us subsequently that, as the suspect workman pounded past the kitchen he had been joined by his companion, who must have come running from the conservatory – later we found the door to Simon's staircase open – and that together they had dashed out of the house. I saw them cut across the flower-bed. From the back they were two thick-set men in dark-blue dungarees; I couldn't have recognized either of them again. They clambered into their van and even before the doors were shut went bowling down the drive. Pursuit would have been useless.

'Your Excellency,' the houseman said.

'Yes?' I turned. 'I'm afraid they've got away, despite your efforts, but it was a good try.'

'Thank you, Your Excellency. I telephoned as you instructed. I was coming to tell you. There were no men scheduled to call on us today.'

I took my cue from Simon. 'I think they were would-be thieves,' I said. 'I'm not surprised the maintenance firm hadn't heard of them.'

'Then the matter should be reported to the police?'

For obvious reasons I didn't want the police. 'I'll see to that,' I said quickly. 'We were lucky this time – they didn't have the opportunity to steal anything – but perhaps we should take it as a warning. In future don't let any workmen into the Residence until you've checked with the place that's meant to have sent them. And keep your eyes open for any strangers in the grounds. You might warn Rule and his wife too.'

'Yes, Your Excellency, I'll do that. But I doubt they'll be back. They weren't local men.'

'How do you know that?'

'They didn't speak French. I supposed they were Flemish but my wife told me they didn't speak Flemish either. They could have come from anywhere. There are so many foreigners in Brussels these days.'

The maintenance men had not been maintenance men. They had not been Belgians. They had not, I was pretty sure, been potential thieves. Simon, sitting on the top stair and hugging his middle, agreed with me. Neither of us wanted to put into words what we both feared.

'If – if,' I said at last, 'they were Russians searching for Baranov, why did they come here?'

Simon shrugged and immediately winced. He tried to smile but it wasn't much of a success. His face was white.

'Are you all right?'

'Sure.'

'Then come down to the study. You'd better have some brandy.'

'At – at eleven in the morning, Lady Rayle?'

'Eleven? Oh, hell!' I said. 'The DCDS! I must get to the airport. Simon – brandy and coffee for you. You're to stay here and look after Baranov. I'll tell them at the office that you're unwell, that you've got some bug or other.

'As you say, Lady Rayle, but – '

'What?'

'I'll do my best. Only – I don't seem much good at unarmed combat. I suppose – you wouldn't have a gun, would you?'

I looked at him. He was serious. I couldn't believe it. He really thought I might have a gun; it must have been because of the professional fashion in which I had dealt with last night's emergency. I hadn't yet told Simon how well briefed I had been by Dick's deputy.

I said: 'Don't worry. They won't come back. Keeping you at home's just a precaution.'

I thought: Thank God Hugo will be here this afternoon. I assumed that Simon was thinking the same thing.

Chapter 9

I telephoned David Driscole and told him I would pick him up in twenty minutes on my way to the airport. In fact it was more like half an hour. He was waiting outside the gates, leaning into the wind, his black hair blown about his face. His expression, as always, was vaguely troubled.

He got into the Rolls and sat beside me, his coldness invading the whole of the car. Involuntarily I shivered. He apologized at once; he was a considerate man but not much use in my present difficulties. And anyway I couldn't involve yet another member of the Mission.

After he had enquired about Simon's sudden indisposition and I had told some suitable lies, we talked shop. He was the only senior member of my staff who ever listened interestedly, without his tongue in his cheek, to my views on détente. He must have wondered why, this morning, I seemed less than enthralled by fresh proofs of communist activity in Europe. Giving him the minimum of attention that courtesy required, I let him ride my hobby-horse for me.

It wasn't until we had almost reached Brussels International that he shocked me into complete concentration.

'Incidentally, Lady Rayle, I've something to ask you,' he said, in his soft, gentle voice. 'I know you're terribly busy today with the DCDS arriving and all that but could you possibly find time to call in at the Hôtel Dieu for a few minutes – perhaps on your way back to the Residence this evening?'

'I expect so,' I said, not hiding my impatience. 'But why, and who's ill, one of the secretaries?'

'If it were merely that I wouldn't bother you,' he said, without implying reproach. 'No, there's a man in the hospital. He's suffering, amongst other things, from a form of amnesia. He doesn't know who he is – or if he does he won't say – and nobody else knows who he is either. He was brought in by a – a friend, who then disappeared. The whole thing's rather odd. The doctors think he was concussed, probably in a car accident. They also think he might be British. Evidently when he's unconscious, which is most of the time, he sometimes babbles in English. His clothes, unfortunately, are "Common Market" and no help. Sir Thomas has been to see him . . .'

'Sir Thomas Bright?'

'Yes. The hospital authorities got in touch with the Embassy and asked if Sir Thomas would visit him. But the result was negative. Sir Thomas could only say that the chap wasn't familiar and, to his knowledge, they had never met.'

'And somebody has now suggested that he might be of interest to the UK Mission to NATO?' I said coldly.

'Sir Thomas thought there might be a chance,' David said, 'or even that it might be – be something personal.'

'How kind of him,' I said. 'Does Sir Thomas usually pass to the Mission problems his Embassy can't deal with?'

David didn't answer that one. It wasn't up to him to adjudicate between me and Tommy Bright. He was doubtless wishing he had gone to the hospital himself and never even mentioned the matter to me. I was still unclear as to why he had; nationals often turn up in casualty wards but are rarely visited by ambassadors. I put the point to David.

'I'm sorry, Lady Rayle,' he said. 'Stupid of me. Sir Thomas went to see him and – and suggested you might be prepared to do the same, because this chap keeps asking for "the British Ambassador". And he's no bum. His body's strong and well cared for, his teeth are good and his nails are manicured. Besides –' David grinned wryly – 'he came in with his pockets stuffed with francs and he's been put in a private room.'

I stared at David, aghast. My indifference to what he had been saying had changed to sudden total interest. An awful possibility had occurred to me. It was just conceivable that the man in the Hôtel Dieu who was so eager to meet the British Ambassador could be Sergei Alexandrov. Indeed, the more I thought of it, the more possible it seemed.

I had heard nothing from Dick's self-styled friend since our telephone conversation last Wednesday, and knew nothing of what he was doing. But he must have realized days ago that, instead of Baranov, he had Sergei on his hands and, if Sergei had become seriously ill, he might have decided to abandon the unfortunate dancer at the hospital. It would have been a rash and stupid thing to do, of course, but perhaps he had had no choice. Certainly, apart from the victim's supposed Englishness, which seemed to have no basis in known fact, there was little to contradict such a hypothesis. Which made it imperative for me to go to the hospital. When, however, was a real problem, with today's programme.

First I had to greet the DCDS and his party; thank God he was an old friend of the UK Military Representative and there had been no question of his staying with me. Then I had to attend the Milrep's luncheon for the honoured guest and be back at NATO by three for a meeting, which I could not cut and which might go on till six. And somehow, in between, I had to sandwich Hugo. My mind jumped – Hugo, Simon, Baranov, the two pseudo-maintenance men, the vulnerability of the Residence, Sergei. Somebody, I thought bitterly, should have told Dick Tindle that being Permanent Representative to the North Atlantic Council was a full-time job and not a side-line to his intelligence work.

'Let the hospital know that I'll visit this man after five,' I said to David.

Pleased, he smiled at me. 'You'd like me to come with you, Lady Rayle?'

'No – no need.' If anybody came with me it would have to be Hugo. 'I shall only be a few minutes. I'm not expecting to recognize him.'

And that at least was true. I didn't know what Sergei looked like. Before I started making desperate telephone calls to Dick I would have to be sure that the man in the hospital bed was Sergei. As to what might happen, should he regain full consciousness in the meantime and declare that he was a dancer from the Bolshoi Ballet Company who had been kidnapped by the British, I was not prepared to think.

I concentrated on being an ambassador.

The Deputy Chief of Defence Staff was charming, and so was his wife. I could have wished them a little less charming. The Milrep had briefed them a little too well. They were determined to be kind to me, to make all allowances. But I was not at my best.

Leaving the airport the official party divided itself between the cars. The DCDS and his aide drove with David and me in the Rolls; the Milrep took the two wives. We were barely seated when the General said:

'Bad show about the Vienna Opera House, isn't it, Lady Rayle?'

I looked at him blankly. 'Has something happened to the Opera House?'

It was his turn to look blank. 'You mean you don't know? I was hoping you might have some later information. Was there nothing in the telegrams?'

'I came straight from the Residence. I've not been into the office yet,' I said, damning David for letting me make what appeared to be a *gaffe* and for doing nothing to save me now, though I glanced at him enquiringly.

The aide said smugly: 'It was in *The Times*, Lady Rayle.'

I had had very little sleep and I had a host of worries. My nerves were screaming with irritability. I didn't care a bloody damn about the Vienna Opera House. I said as much, acidly.

'I'm afraid I've had more important things to occupy me this morning.'

'But – but, my dear lady!'

'Perhaps you would be good enough to enlighten me, General.'

'Yes, of course,' he said, and began to explain. 'Yesterday afternoon a left-wing group – they call themselves "Fighters for Free Austria", but no doubt they're inspired and financed from Moscow – seized the Opera House and some of the cast of *Figaro*, who happened to be rehearsing at the time. They threatened to burn down the place, and the hostages with it, if some political prisoners weren't released before a certain deadline today. The Government didn't wait for any deadline. They sent in their new riot squad. My latest information is that the place is on fire and more than a dozen people killed. That's bad enough, God knows.' He shook his head sadly. 'But it's the implications which are important, dear lady, the implications.'

'I appreciate that,' I said, thinking of Dick Tindle's prophecy about Austria.

'There's going to be trouble, big trouble in the New Year when the Austrians hold their elections. The left is becoming a real threat and if the USSR . . .'

I listened to him with a show of attention; it was the least I could do. But he had nothing interesting to add and he certainly didn't want to hear my views. In the circumstances I couldn't blame him.

Any other morning, I thought ruefully, I would have read the story in the London papers, which I saw at the office, and Simon would have been bursting with the news; but today neither he nor I . . . As for David Driscole, he had assumed my prior knowledge, reasonably enough, and in fact his references to Austria on the way to the airport now made more sense to me than they had then, when my mind had been on Baranov.

Baranov! I sighed. Things were getting on top of me. At the present moment, whatever it did for my ambassadorial image, I simply couldn't afford to concern myself with the Vienna Opera House or Austrian elections or anything but Dick Tindle's affairs – not as long as Baranov remained an unwanted guest at the Residence.

The food and wine had been excellent, but too much for the middle of the day. I drank cup after cup of black coffee. Back in the office I took some aspirin and told my secretary that I wasn't to be disturbed until it was time for the meeting. I sat across my desk from Hugo. Beginning with my telephone conversation with Dick's deputy, I told him everything that had happened since Saturday morning. I hadn't realized that there was such a lot.

'My dear Kit, what fun and games you've been having,' he said.

'I'd happily have done without them.'

He grinned at me. Obviously his weekend in Paris had done him good. He was far more relaxed and cheerful than when he went. He and Daphne must have enjoyed themselves and, if so, they had been luckier than I had. I felt a sudden twinge of envy, recalling the past, not with Hugo but with Guy.

'I was hoping you'd make some constructive comments,' I said.

'I'll try, though you seem to have done perfectly well without me.' He leaned back in his chair and crossed one leg over the other. 'The really important thing is the business of those maintenance men this morning – if they were Russians. And we must assume they were. Kit, I think you should mention it to people. Tell everyone at your reception for the DCDS tonight how you and Simon foiled some would-be burglars. That's what anybody who was not hiding Baranov would do. Then with luck the news will trickle along the grapevine to the Russian Embassy and, we hope, dampen any suspicions of you and the Residence. It's possible they were only checking. In their position I'd certainly be doing my best to check, on the Israelis – they'll know by now that Marika has defected too – the Americans and the British, in that order. I'll try to find out if anyone else has had any odd workmen.'

'And if they haven't?'

'We'll have to accept that, somehow, the Russians knew it was us. But God knows what we do then – except watch and pray.'

The buzzer on my intercom made frantic noises. I had been ignoring its more gentle reminders for the past five minutes. My watch showed three o'clock. I pressed the switch.

'Lady Rayle, your meeting –'

'Coming,' I said into the squawk box, and to Hugo: 'Sorry, I really must go. I'll see you this evening. I suppose you don't want to come to the hospital with me?'

'No. It's too much for both the ambassador and the minister to visit an unknown patient. And if by some unlikely chance he does turn out to be Sergei, we don't want to draw attention to him.'

I stood up and collected the papers I needed for the meeting. 'You don't believe it's Sergei, do you? You think someone would have been sure to mention the bullet-wound?'

Hugo shrugged. 'I should be exceedingly surprised if it were. I admit the set-up's peculiar but we can't blame Dick Tindle for every peculiar thing that happens in Brussels, can we? That would be obsessive.'

This was the first acid remark that Hugo had made about Dick during the whole of our discussion. I had expected him to argue violently – as Simon had yearned to do – against taking Baranov to the Secretary General before consultation with the Office, but he had let it go. He hadn't argued at all. He had accepted blithely that whatever Dick Tindle wanted was what should be. And, even though I had been thankful for it, I had found this change of heart more than a little disconcerting. Now he had reverted to the old Hugo.

Opening the door and letting me pass into the room that was usually occupied by Simon, he said:

'Incidentally your dear Dick's damn lucky he's not going to have to bail me out of prison.'

'What do you mean?'

'I phoned Lena as soon as I got back from Paris. I had to find out what had happened about the Mercedes. After all, I've got a personal interest. She told me that the Russians have been putting a lot of pressure on the police to find out who killed their KGB boy. The police – full of apologies for disturbing the great man, of course – were actually waiting to question her boy-friend when he returned from his in-laws on Sunday night. In turn, he asked her a few pointed questions. She had quite a time with him.'

'Is everything all right now?'

'Yes, I hope so. Nobody can afford to lean too heavily on the next chap. In the end they'll have to agree that the car was stolen by a person or persons unknown. But it's no thanks to Dick Tindle and his friends, is it?'

They talked and talked. I thought the bloody meeting would never end. Finally, at five-forty, when I was feeling desperate, the Chairman decided to pack it in. I thrust my papers, mostly consisting of doodles, into a briefcase and, by-passing the polite chit-chat that seems to form a postscript to most NATO meetings, hurried from the conference room, along the unending claustrophobic corridors, back to my office. My secretary was still there, typing the draft of my speech to the Atlantic Assembly.

'Tell Rule I want the car immediately,' I said. 'Then you go home. That typing can wait till morning.'

She smiled her thanks. 'The Minister left you this note and packet, Lady Rayle. He said you were to be sure to read the note before you went to the hospital. It's about the flowers.'

Flowers, for Sergei? Of course I should have thought of flowers. They were the natural thing to take to anyone in hospital. I tore the envelope open on my way through to my room. Hugo, with his usual foresight, had arranged for me to collect some chrysanthemums from La Belle Marguerite, the shop that supplied the Residence. Nor was it the only thing he had arranged.

The note read: '. . . if there's a thousand to one chance that we have found S, use the attached. Love. Hugo.'

Asking myself what else I had forgotten, I picked up the packet from my desk. It was small, oblong, fairly heavy, and contained a camera. This was something I would never have thought of. I slipped the camera into my handbag, made sure the safe was locked and there were no papers lying about, and seized my coat. I almost ran down the corridor to the entrance hall in the centre of the building.

Nevertheless, it was six o'clock as, driving through the gates, I acknowledged the guard's salute. Hugo, who always thought of everything, had overlooked one thing – the time. The rush-hour was at its peak, the traffic heavy, and, when we reached La Belle Marguerite, the shop was shut. I swore.

Even with an ambassador's car there's a limit to what one can do. The street in which the Marguerite is situated is narrow and invariably congested. This evening the traffic was competing with the proverbial snail. And already there were impatient hoots behind us. I was in two minds about abandoning the flowers. But I told Rule to drive round the block while I hammered on the glass and tried to persuade the girl sweeping the floor to open the door to me. Eventually I succeeded and, clutching a great bunch of bronze chrysanthemums, stood on the pavement and willed Rule to return.

He came at last and our luck seemed to change. The traffic

was thinner, the lights accommodated us, and we had no problem parking at the Hôtel Dieu. There, my name was immediately recognized at the reception desk; David Driscole had done his stuff, perhaps too well. I should have been happier without the red-carpet treatment. It involved me in an interview with Matron herself and I had to hear how *le pauvre* had been left in the waiting-room of the Emergency Department at the busiest period of Saturday night. It had been some time before the sister on duty had realized he was a patient and not a relative. Subsequently he had been given the best possible treatment. None of this information was any use to me but, as I had agreed with Hugo, I refrained from asking questions.

'If I could just see him,' I said. 'Maybe talk to him for a few minutes.'

Matron took the hint. A young nurse was summoned and I was taken along wide green passages, up in a lift and along more green passages. Everywhere there was an air of quiet bustle; patients were being fed and tidied and made ready for the evening visiting hours. The smells of food, flowers, ether, anxiety, antiseptic mingled with the sounds of hurrying footsteps, bells, rubber-wheeled trolleys, crockery, muted voices and, behind a closed door, somebody sobbing. It was like thousands of other hospitals across the world.

Over the years, out of love or friendship or duty, I had visited my share of such places. But never before had I felt so nervous. I told myself that I had to be wrong. *Le pauvre* whom I was about to see could not be Sergei Alexandrov.

The nurse stood aside to let me go into the room. 'Mostly he sleeps,' she said in bad French, 'and sometimes in his half-sleep he talks – in different languages but often in English. When he wakes he does not talk, except for a word or two. Repeatedly he says, "British Ambassador". It's not much.' She looked up at me with great earnestness; she was a short, stolid Flemish girl, not very attractive. 'He's a good man, a kind man. Try to help him, madame, please.'

Before I could answer, she had whisked the chrysanthemums from my grasp and was gone. I walked across to the bed. The 'good, kind man' was lying flat on his back, asleep, his toes making twin peaks under the blanket, his large hands folded loosely outside the coverlet. His face, good-looking in a craggy kind of way, was drawn with pain. His head was bandaged so that it was impossible to see the colour of his hair, but his eyebrows were reddish-brown. From the breadth of his shoulders in the white cotton operating-gown and the mound of his body under the bedclothes it was obvious that he was physically very big indeed. Whatever else he might be he was not a ballet dancer. He was not Sergei Alexandrov.

I sank into the bedside chair. I was overcome with relief. If the patient had been Sergei – and I had been so afraid that it might be – he would have posed innumerable problems. Now I didn't have to worry about him. I found myself grinning inanely at the still, pale face. I was sick with anti-climax.

'British,' he said suddenly, loudly. 'British Ambassador. I insist. Urgent.' His voice faded. He was asleep.

He had made me jump and, gripping my handbag, I felt the hard outline of the camera that Hugo had provided. On an impulse I took it out. It was a Polaroid model so there was no bother. I took a photograph of the patient's head and shoulders, waited to make sure the print was adequate, and then took another of his length in the bed.

'Who the devil are you?' the man said.

He was awake and fully conscious. His eyes, deep set, were an unusual shade of grey, the colour of slate. They didn't waver as he stared at me. I could feel his hostility. His hand was on the bell-push.

'I'm Catherine Rayle,' I said. 'I'm the British Permament Representative – the British Ambassador to NATO.'

'Catherine Rayle, British Ambassador,' he said.

His eyes lost their coldness, his body relaxed and he took his hand from the bell. He smiled at me and deep clefts appeared in his cheeks. I understood why the nurse had found him so appealing.

'British Ambassador,' he said again.

'Yes,' I said. 'Who are you? What's your name?'

'Lady,' he said. 'Lady – '

He tried to sit up, failed, and sank back on the pillows, his eyes closed. The nurse returned with my flowers in a vase. I told her that he had spoken and had seemed lucid for a couple of minutes but she wasn't impressed; it wasn't anything new. She was disappointed that there was nothing about him I had recognized, that my visit had been futile. I couldn't tell her that as far as I was concerned the visit had achieved its purpose. Her patient, thank God, was not Sergei; though I was sorry for him, he was no concern of mine.

Instead I said goodbye and, curled up on the back seat of the Rolls, slept all the way to the Residence. I needed that sleep.

Chapter 10

My reception for the Deputy Chief of Defence Staff was one of those protocol affairs that demand nothing except good caterers, the guests of honour and perhaps, as an afterthought, the presence of the hostess. I just made it.

I had twenty minutes to spare when Rule, shaking me by the shoulder, woke me from a dead sleep. Simon, who had been on the look-out for the Rolls, was waiting at the front door. I ran past him and up the stairs. I stopped on the threshold of my bedroom. Simon was breathing down my neck.

'Is everything all right?'

'Yes, Lady Rayle. No more excitements. I asked Cook for a special lunch, said I'd have it upstairs, and whisked it along, hot, to Baranov. It cheered him up. We've been playing chess.'

'Good. You'd better spend the evening with him.'

'But what about the reception? I told Polly – '

'For half an hour. You're meant to be ill, remember.'

'Yes, Lady Rayle.' He heaved a gusty sigh. 'Hugo dropped in and – '

'Later.' I was shutting the door on him.

' – think you should know.' Simon had raised his voice.

'What?' I opened the door again.

'Two things, Lady Rayle. First, Hugo dropped in about six and insisted on seeing Baranov by himself. Second, Cook says the maintenance man who was in the kitchen asked her who lived in the Residence and – and if you had any house-guests.'

I nodded, hearing what Simon said but not really paying attention. 'Later,' I repeated firmly and shut the door. For a moment I leaned against it, my mind a blank, then I pulled myself together. In a flurry of skirt, shirt, pants and bra I was naked, my discarded clothes making a trail to the bathroom.

For three minutes I luxuriated under the shower. It made a new woman of me. And, some quarter of an hour later, standing at the head of the reception line as I welcomed my guests, I felt calm, cool and collected, and reasonably sure that the stresses of the last few days weren't showing beneath, like a dirty slip.

I shook hands, smiled, made greeting noises and presented to the DCDS the few people whom he didn't already know. This was something I was good at. A natural talent for remembering names and interests – the sort of thing that can make the briefest of encounters personal – had been burnished by my years as an MP's wife. Tonight, however, I needed to concentrate.

Hugo and Daphne, doing their duty by arriving early, should have provided a moment or two's respite but, in fact, only reminded me of the real problems. Daphne had heard the story of my 'maintenance men' from Hugo and seemed to be intrigued by it. Her curiosity gave him an opportunity to tell me that nobody else, as far as he knew, had had suspect workmen. And, while I frowned over the implications of that and Daphne chatted to the DCDS, he said:

'You got to the hospital, Kit?'

'Yes,' I said, 'and you were right. It was a waste of time.'

'Thank God for that,' he said. 'At least it's one thing less to worry about.'

More guests were announced. Hugo, giving me a half-hearted smile, began to move along the line of VIPs. The reception was getting under way. The roar of conversation, interspersed with laughter and the cheerful noise of ice-cubes clicking against glass, maintained a steady level. Drink and food were circulating. The party was going well.

I turned at a touch on my elbow. The houseman was hovering behind me. 'Your Excellency is wanted on the telephone,' he murmured.

It had to be important, otherwise he would never have interrupted me at such a time. Nevertheless, I couldn't take the call now; he should surely have realized that.

'Tell whoever it is to leave a message or to phone again in an hour or so,' I said and turned back to greet the Belgian Minister of Defence.

Chatting with the Minister, I became aware of the houseman's continued presence. He had withdrawn a step or two but was still waiting his chance to speak to me. He hadn't gone to do as I asked. Slowly, while the Minister paid me elaborate compliments, my smile began to congeal and my eyes to glaze. The importance of the telephone call, of the waiting listener about to put down the receiver before I could answer, loomed larger and larger.

But finally the moment came when the Minister moved on to the DCDS. The houseman wasted no more time. He was quick and brief. 'I was to tell you it is *l'ami de Dick*, Your Excellency,' he said.

I swallowed my half-articulated and wholly unnecessary 'Who?' It was stupid to pretend. God knows what the damned man had said to him but the houseman was obviously aware that the name would have meaning for me. As I hurried to the study I asked myself what else he and his wife either knew or guessed. They weren't fools and, although their quarters were to a great extent isolated in one wing of the house, they probably had a good idea that someone was living in the major guest suite. What they would have no reason to suspect, however, was that the someone was Baranov, unless . . .

I controlled my wild thoughts, picked up the receiver, said: 'Lady Rayle speaking.' And at once I heard the disconnecting click as the telephone in the servants' hall was replaced. Now I could only hear quick breathing. 'Hullo, this is Catherine Rayle.'

'Lady Rayle, it is Dick's friend here. You remember me, I am sure. My apologies for not having got in touch with you as I promised. But things have gone wrong, badly wrong.'

It was the same voice, the same verbosity, the same impossible accent. This time, however, nervousness swamped his self-importance. He generated a feeling of crisis.

Personally I don't believe in premonitions but if ever I had one it was then. As he rambled on, saying that he had done his best, that without instructions and without the Captain no more was possible, that the mistakes were not his responsibility, that he was no longer safe where he was, that he intended to leave the country tonight, I knew that he was spelling out disaster. And

I knew that, whatever I did, I wouldn't be able to prevent it.

'You must tell Dick all I have said, Lady Rayle, so that he understands the blame is not mine. As for the parcel I was to deliver to you, it was damaged and anyway not the right parcel but none the less I bring it to you, to the – the glass annexe.'

'No!' I said, horrified as I grasped what he meant. 'I – I don't want it.'

'You have the other parcel, the right one?'

'Yes.' I could have bitten my tongue. 'How – how did you know that?'

'I read the newspapers. I reason that if there is no excitement about the parcel I have, perhaps the other also is lost and you have it,' he said simply. It was clear, logical thinking.

'That was clever of you,' I said. I was surprised at the calmness of my voice. 'And you are right. I have what Dick wanted me to have, which makes it very important that you should not send me the other parcel. Dick would not –'

'Lady Rayle, you do not understand. There is no choice. You have both parcels whether you like it or not.'

'Now listen,' I said sharply, allowing my irritation to show.

I forced myself to think – there had to be some argument to convince him that I couldn't cope with Sergei as well as Baranov – but it was a wasted effort. He was a weak man with all a weak man's stubbornness, and the only card I had to play was Dick. I began to reiterate that Dick wouldn't want the second parcel brought to me when again he interrupted. He wouldn't even hear me out.

'There is no question, Lady Rayle, so please do not argue. Already it is arranged,' he said. 'I am sorry about it, truly sorry, but Dick will understand. And for my own sake I must go. Goodbye, Lady Rayle.'

'Wait!' I said. 'Wait! You haven't told me –'

But the line was dead. I stared in stupefaction at the telephone. I couldn't believe it; Sergei was going to be delivered to the Residence and I didn't know when or where or how. God damn Dick Tindle! In a burst of useless temper I banged the receiver on to its stand.

I went back to the reception. What else was there to do?

Luckily it was easy; it was my party, but the guests, mostly military, were here to meet the DCDS and – cynical thought – each other. I was a supernumerary. I looked for Hugo, who was deep in conversation with the Norwegian Milrep. I would have to make an opportunity to tell him about Sergei. Simon too would have to be warned. Simon had not yet appeared.

Pursuing my own preoccupations I continued to play the hostess. In due time the crowd began to thin. I shook hands, made the right responses, wished they would all go. Tiredness had crept up on me again.

The Brights came to say goodbye, Polly appearing disconsolate; I hoped she wasn't thinking of sneaking a quick visit to Simon. Hugo and Daphne were just behind them. Sir Thomas fell back to have a word with Hugo – I heard him mention something about Austria – and I shook Daphne's limp hand. I didn't notice Simon until Polly gasped.

'Simon!'

'Good – good evening.'

'My dear boy,' from Lady Bright, 'you do look unwell.'

Polly was more outspoken. 'Simon, you look ghastly.'

And Daphne more unkind. 'You're pea-green, Simon.' She laughed, her little tinkling laugh.

The two men stopped talking and we all regarded the unfortunate Simon, not least Hugo and I who knew that nothing had been wrong with him earlier, that his 'indisposition' had been tactical. My first reaction was that he had made himself up for the part of invalid and had overdone it. But this was no fake; he wasn't putting it on. He was ill.

'Lady Rayle.'

Simon, I realized at once, had come downstairs because he needed to speak to me, not to the Brights, not even to Polly, and certainly not to Daphne. He was unlucky to find us all in a cluster. He had to make a stupendous effort to appear normal, and he wasn't being very successful.

He stood in front of us, holding himself artificially erect and determined not to sway. He tried to smile; the smile was a mere stretching of the lower face and never reached his eyes, which were very bright and not quite focused. He passed his tongue over his lips. His supercilious nose wrinkled; he must have tasted the sweat that was shimmering on his skin because, with a clumsy gesture, he thrust his hand into his trouser pocket, pulled out a handkerchief and was about to wipe his mouth.

'Simon!' Polly said again.

For a lengthening moment Simon stared at the handkerchief. It was made of fine white linen, monogrammed in one corner, the sort of expensive item that people give as presents but that the fastidious Simon would buy for himself. It was splotched with clear, fresh blood.

Simon smiled foolishly. Then his eyes rolled up in their sockets and he folded to the floor. Hugo had forestalled him enough to break the fall and the carpet was thick. He made little more than a heavy thud.

Conversation in the room faded and immediately regathered strength. The American Permament Representative and his colleague, who had been waiting to say goodbye to me, asked if they could help, but Hugo and Tommy Bright were already carrying Simon out. Polly picked up the blood-stained handkerchief and tried to stuff it into her too-small bag.

'Perhaps – perhaps he had a nose-bleed,' she said.

'A bloody nose and he faints? Poor Simon!' Daphne said.

Polly was quick to defend him. 'There are a lot of people like that, who can't stand the sight of blood,' she said fiercely. 'They can't help it. It's nothing to sneer at.'

'Polly!' Lady Bright warned, but, as she turned to me, her smile excluded Daphne. 'Catherine, my dear, thank you very much. We'll wait for Tommy in the car.'

'I shan't wait for Hugo,' Daphne said, after Lady Bright had gone, taking a reluctant Polly with her. 'He can walk up through the garden. After all, he knows his way very well from one to other of us, doesn't he, Catherine?'

I didn't answer. I yearned to pick Daphne Pewter up and shake her, like an unloved doll; but this was neither the time nor the place. I said goodbye to the two Americans and to a succession of my guests. As so often happens once a party starts to break up, everyone began to leave. Our gathering was soon reduced to the DCDS and his immediate circle. Sir Thomas Bright reappeared.

'How is Simon?'

'Just a faint. He took a while to come out of it but he'll be all right.'

'Thank you for helping, Tommy.'

'My dear . . . I rather think Simon's to be my future son-in-law, though I'm not meant to know that yet.'

'He's lucky,' I said, 'and so are you.'

'I expect you're right. He should do well. But a career diplomat should always watch his step. I'm afraid that Simon may be a little too – adventurous for his own good, and Polly's.' Sir Thomas looked me straight in the eye. '*Au 'voir*, my dear. Lovely party, as always,' he said.

Thankfully I saw that the DCDS and the last of my guests were about to leave.

I found Hugo and Simon in the study. Simon was lying on the settee with a glass of brandy in his hand. There was colour in his cheeks and he no longer looked ill. Of the two of them Hugo was now the more visibly upset. He had been walking up and down the room as I came in, and when I shut the door he resumed his pacing.

'Go on!' he said to Simon.

'Lady Rayle, I'm terribly sorry,' Simon said. 'It was the blood, all over my hands. I know it's stupid but I've always been like that.'

'For God's sake!' Hugo said through his teeth. 'Forget the blood. Go on with what you were telling me. You heard a scrabbling noise in the conservatory and went to see what it was.'

'And when I came to – the second time, that is – I didn't realize Tommy, Sir Thomas, was here,' Simon continued, speaking to me and ignoring Hugo. 'I just saw Hugo and I said: "Hugo, I've found a Russian in the conservatory." It must have sounded crazy. Lord knows what Tommy thought.'

Hugo groaned aloud. 'There's nobody there now,' he said to me. 'I've been to look. What happened next, Simon? Did you have a fight with the Russian?'

'No. Oh no!' Simon laughed. The brandy, on top of shock, was having its effect. 'You see, this numero was lying on the ground, behind some potted plants. He was wrapped in a blanket like a mummy. He couldn't move but he mumbled at me – in Russian. I didn't really understand. Still, it was clear he was in a bad way and needed help.' Simon's voice slurred. 'I couldn't leave him there, could I? Anybody could have come along.'

Simon lifted the glass he was holding. Before Hugo could prise it from him he had drunk seven-eighths of the brandy that remained. The last eighth trickled down his chin. His head nodded. His eyelids began to droop. I gasped as Hugo slapped him across the face.

'Wake up, you drunken sod!'

Simon opened his eyes wide. Spacing each word carefully, he said: 'Don't ever t – touch me again – sir!'

'What – what did you do with the Russian, Simon?'

'I carried him up to my rooms, Lady Rayle. He's a smallish man but he's not light and I had a lot of trouble on those winding stairs. Perhaps it was my fault. I don't know. Anyway, I think he's been hurt. He'd got a great bandage. Maybe something broke open. Because when I put him down there was – was blood on him and me and, I'm sorry, I passed out. As soon as I could – I had to change my suit – I came to find you.'

I nodded. Words stuck in my throat. The man whom Simon had found in the conservatory, the 'glass annexe' as Dick's friend had called it, was obviously Sergei Alexandrov. Only last week he had been dancing with Baranov and the Bolshoi Company, and now . . . Telling Simon to stay where he was, I hurried after Hugo, who had disappeared from the room even before Simon had finished speaking.

In the hall the houseman stopped me. He wanted to know what I and Mr Maryton and my guests – my guests? – required for supper. With a tremendous effort of will he tried to keep his eyes from flicking up the stairs; doubtless he had just seen Hugo taking them two at a time.

I heard myself say: 'Soup, an omelette, some cheese and fruit. And coffee – lots of coffee. For three. Mr Pewter will be staying.' The words sounded meaningless, absurd.

'In a half-hour, Your Excellency,' he said, and watched me follow Hugo.

I ran. The houseman could think what he damn well liked. The important thing was to get to Sergei. My mind closed, refusing to accept the bloody picture that Simon had conjured. And, in the event, the reality was not gruesome.

Sergei Alexandrov lay flat on his back on the floor of Simon's bedroom, his arms parallel to his sides, his toes pointing towards the ceiling, his head supported by a cushion. He was wearing black suede shoes, black trousers, a blue shirt open at the neck, and a leather jacket. He was still partially wrapped in the blanket in which he had been delivered and on the blanket were patches of dried blood. There was also a thin trickle of black blood from one side of his mouth into the hollow of his neck, and his shirt was discoloured. Underneath it, however, the bandages around his shoulder and part of his chest seemed unstained. Simon had been wrong. Sergei's gunshot wound had not broken open; the blood hadn't come from there.

'How is he, Hugo?'

'I'm not – not sure.'

Hugo got up rather stiffly from where he had been kneeling beside Sergei and, without so much as a glance at me, went into the adjoining bathroom. I could hear him opening cupboards and drawers, rummaging in them and banging them shut again, as if he were searching for something.

'What is it? What are you doing?' I asked.

'Wait a minute, Kit!' He was impatient.

I looked down at Sergei's still face, the high Slavic cheekbones, the concave cheeks, the waxen pallor that reminded me of Guy when he was . . . I went into the bathroom.

'Hugo, we must get a doctor. If we don't Sergei may – '

'Sergei? Of course!' Hugo said. 'I should have worked that out for myself.'

I explained about the telephone call I'd had – I'd forgotten that Hugo hadn't known the identity of the injured man – and he cursed, softly and bitterly.

'Nobody,' he said, 'nobody has the right to play with other

people's lives as General Sir Richard Tindle's prepared to do.'

By now he had found what he wanted, one of those small rectangular mirrors that are part of the fittings of more expensive handbags. I have no idea what use Simon made of it. Hugo's purpose was only too clear.

We went back into the bedroom and knelt, one on either side of Sergei, and Hugo held the mirror over the Russian's mouth and nostrils.

'There's no pulse and no heartbeat, Kit.'

'But he can't be – Oh no! Please God, no!'

Hugo turned the mirror so that I could see its other side; the glass was unclouded. 'You'd better save your prayers for us,' he said gently. 'Sergei's dead.'

He reached for the two sides of the blanket on which Sergei was lying and folded them over the body. I was already thinking of it as 'the body' but half my mind laughed at my own stupidity. Sergei could not be dead.

'How – ' I began. 'How did he die? And where's all the blood that upset Simon?'

Hugo went into the bathroom, I thought to put away the mirror. He returned carrying the jacket of the suit that Simon had discarded before he came down to the reception. A big, dark blotch stained the lower half of the back.

'Blood,' Hugo said. 'A lot of it. There's more on the seat of the trousers. Sergei must have had some kind of internal hæmorrhage as Simon was carrying him upstairs in a fireman's lift. That's probably when he died.'

'Poor Sergei!' I said with pity. 'What a stupid way to die.'

'Better than alone among the potted plants,' Hugo said blackly.

I shook my head. 'I meant it shouldn't have happened to him at all. He was just a – a bystander, a friend of Baranov's. He got involved by mistake.' I shivered.

Hugo put his arm around my waist and for a moment held me close to him. 'Dearest Kit,' he murmured, 'this is no time for philosophizing.'

For a moment I clung to him, taking comfort from his hard, male strength. Then I pulled away. This was no time for dalliance either. Hugo grinned at me; he had guessed what I was thinking. 'Let's go next door and drink some of Simon's whisky,' he said.

'Oughtn't we to telephone the police? We can't leave it too long,' I said. 'They'll be able to tell more or less when he died.'

Hugo didn't answer at once. He went into the sitting-room, leaving me to follow him, and poured two stiff whiskies from the decanter. I collapsed into Simon's most comfortable chair and put my feet up on the foot-stool. I felt exhausted, mentally and physically. My hump ached. But slowly my brain began to tick again.

'What – what are we going to say to the police?' I said.

Hugo sipped his whisky and made a helpless sort of gesture. 'What do you suggest?' he said.

'The truth, I suppose, or a version of it. We found Sergei in the conservatory. We'd never seen him before. He was – '

'Oh, for Chrissakes!' Hugo said. 'Don't be so naïve, Kit. You're living in the real world now, not in Oxford's ivory towers.'

'All right!' I made an effort to control my temper. 'I admit I'm not used to this sort of thing. What does the Minister advise?'

Hugo gave me a sour smile. I didn't blame him. I knew I was being bitchy. I took a deep breath and got control of myself. I said:

'Hugo, I'm sorry. This is an unbelievable situation and I'm out of my depth. Please help.'

'Of course,' he said. 'Hugo to the rescue – exactly as your dear Dick foresaw. If I didn't loathe his guts I'd admire the bloody man.'

'You think we should try to phone Dick?'

'What for? He won't be able to help. Isn't it obvious his Brussels people have broken down? Otherwise they'd never have dumped Sergei on you like this. And there isn't time for him to organize anyone else. The crisis is here and now.' Hugo passed a hand over his face. 'I'm sorry too, Kit. But I'm supposed to be a diplomat – not 007. And this is a hell of a mess.'

'We'll have to call the police,' I said.

'We can't!' Hugo said. 'There'd be an appalling outcry. The Russians would swear to high heaven that the Brits had kidnapped Sergei and that he'd been killed trying to escape. They'd demand "justice". Oh, I don't suppose that you or I – or Simon for that matter – would spend the rest of our days in a Belgian prison, but there'd be a dreadful stink. The Russians would make the most of it. They always do.'

'There's Baranov to consider too,' I said, suddenly remembering. Any scandal about us and Sergei is going to make his information suspect, isn't it?'

'Yes.'

I gave Hugo a sharp glance but he was staring into his whisky. He opened his mouth and shut it again. I had the distinct impression that he'd been about to say something important, but had changed his mind.

'Hugo, Dick's deputy impressed on me how much Baranov's information mattered. He said it was vital. We can't do anything to damage its credibility.'

'No, Kit. I was waiting for you to get around to that.' Hugo drained his glass. He stood up. 'My dear, there's only one answer. For your sake and my sake and Simon's sake, not to mention British prestige and Tindle's little plans, Sergei's body must disappear.'

Chapter 11

It was after midnight.

There were four of us in the conservatory, Hugo, Simon, myself and the dead Russian. Through the glass we could see the grounds, secret and full of racing shadows. A puny moon played hide and seek among the black clouds. The wind was high; it whispered among the grass and fallen leaves and made the whole garden live. But it was keeping off the rain, which was a blessing.

'I do wish you'd let me come with you, Lady Rayle,' Simon said.

'No,' I said.

Simon had slept off the shock and the brandy and was eager to make amends for his earlier weakness. The fact that Sergei was dead didn't seem to bother him unduly. He had insisted on carrying the body down the narrow, winding stairs to the conservatory, handling it in the most casual fashion as if it really were the parcel that Dick Tindle's people called it. Evidently it was only blood that threw Simon.

Hugo and I were far more affected. Hugo, who had forced himself – needlessly as it turned out – to undress and redress Sergei in case some message had been attached to his clothing, obviously hated what we were doing. And I shared his feelings. Nevertheless, especially after Tommy Bright's comments, I refused to commit Simon to what was without question an indefensible, criminal act. Hugo and I would have to control our queasiness and cope by ourselves.

'At least let me help carry him as far as the car, Lady Rayle,' Simon insisted. 'You'll have enough carrying at the other end.'

'No,' I said. 'You've got to stay with Baranov, as we agreed. You ought to be with him now.'

'But as you are here,' Hugo said wearily, 'for God's sake stop arguing and get Sergei fixed or we'll never start on this woeful expedition.'

The expedition, of course, was to dispose of the body. We had decided that there was no alternative to doing this – and to doing it without the Russians' knowledge. We had to assume the Residence was watched; otherwise Hugo could have brought his car to the front door and we could have driven boldly down the drive with Sergei in the boot or under a rug on the back seat. The trouble was that the road in front of the house was usually lined with parked cars, and the Russians could be in any one of them; they would undoubtedly follow any vehicle emerging from our driveway at this time of night, after the guests had gone.

Fortunately the dead-end lane behind the Residence was too narrow for even the smallest car, and a watcher there would be obvious. Surveillance of one residence by members of another mission is not exactly in accordance with diplomatic practice and we calculated that the Russians would not want to risk interrogation by a passing patrol. The best they could do at the back was to station a vehicle near where the lane sidled into a quiet street. If we could get Sergei across the lane and into the garden of the Pewters' house without drawing attention to ourselves we stood a chance of evading them.

Thus we had no choice but to attempt to carry the body up to the lane, though both the houseman's quarters and the Rules' flat above the garage overlooked our route through the grounds; if one of the Rules couldn't sleep or the houseman or his wife had an excess of curiosity, they would have an excellent view of the proceedings. We had decided, therefore, on a little deception.

First Hugo and I took hold of each other's wrists to make a traditional three-handed lift. Simon pushed Sergei on to this improvised seat, and Hugo used his spare hand to support the body from behind. Next Simon pinned the sleeves of Sergei's jacket so that one of Sergei's arms was round my shoulders and one round Hugo's. In the uncertain moonlight, we hoped it looked as if Simon and I were helping home a drunken Hugo by the most discreet path. It was not a normal occurrence, as Hugo had pointed out sardonically, but it was not totally implausible. And the circumstances would make the chauffeur and the houseman think twice before coming out to investigate more closely.

When this plan was suggested it had seemed a good idea. My enthusiasm was short-lived, however. There was all the difference in the world between a warm, pulsing drunk and a corpse. Even the weight of Sergei's arm across my shoulders and the feel of his bony buttocks on my hands made me want to shiver. And there were practical problems. He was much heavier than we had expected and he tended to slide off his seat. With only one hand available, Hugo had trouble holding him in place. Soon, in spite of the cold, we were both sweating.

To shorten the portage we left the gravel path and cut across the grass. This was a mistake. The rough ground made our going uneven and Hugo found it impossible to keep Sergei upright. Suddenly, as cloud covered the moon, the body slipped from his grasp. At the same time I turned my ankle, stumbled and fell. The side of Sergei's face brushed against my mouth. I wanted to be sick. I gulped the clean wind.

'All right, Kit?'

'Yes. And you?'

'Yes. But the pins have torn out of his jacket.'

After that we carried him a different way. I went first, holding an ankle in each hand; Hugo supported him under the arms. This was easier for me, but Hugo, who had to bear four-fifths of the weight, began to gasp for breath. We had to stop again.

'Too much liquor and not enough exercise,' Hugo said, breathing hard.

It was then I had a bright idea. Leaving Hugo to recover, I hurried through the darkness and the night to the garden shed. I forgot the torch in my pocket and found the wheelbarrow by bruising my shins on it. The damned thing was stacked high with flowerpots. Cursing, I began to unload them and somehow I let one slip. In the juggling act to save it I knocked a rake off the wall. The noise seemed appalling.

Speed was clearly more important now than silence. I got out of the shed, kicked the door shut behind me and trundled the wheelbarrow back to the shrubbery as fast as I could.

'What the hell have you been doing?' Hugo said angrily.

'Sorry,' I said, knowing he didn't want an explanation.

We wasted no more time. Lifting Sergei between us, we tried to put him in the wheelbarrow. But, to my chagrin, it wasn't possible. He wouldn't fit – not until we had forced his stiffening limbs into a foetal position. It was a disgusting thing to have to do. As together we pushed the wheelbarrow up the rest of the hill to the lane, I wondered how much more of this Hugo and I could take.

The lane was deserted. There was nobody walking a dog, nobody pretending to relieve himself against a tree. But I was thankful when we reached the dead-end and the back entrance to the Pewters' garden, with its promise of security. The respite was short.

'Wait here,' Hugo said. 'I'll back up the car as far as I can.'

I stood in the shelter of some shrubs, envying Daphne in the sleeping house, and felt myself overwhelmed by a sudden loneliness. Time stretched. The wind whipped a scurry of leaves around my ankles. And whipped the clouds across the moon so that the interplay of light and dark terrified my imagination. I never heard the car. Hugo was standing beside me.

'Come on, Kit,' he said impatiently. 'The sooner we get this over, the better.'

The next bit wasn't too difficult. Sergei was not a big man and, as he was now shaped, he fitted easily into the Rover; Hugo had thoughtfully lined the boot with newspaper. We left the wheelbarrow in the shrubs – Hugo would bring it back to the Residence early tomorrow – and drove sombrely down the drive. When we reached the road Hugo switched on the car lights. We didn't hurry; we went very carefully, criss-crossing the quiet streets as if we were going home from a late party. Nobody followed us. Nobody showed the least interest in us. The Russians presumably continued their watch on the Residence, and we headed south-east out of Brussels.

We took the Route de Mont-Saint-Jean, which runs for ten miles straight through the Forêt de Soignes to the battlefield of Waterloo. In the small hours of such a wild night we hadn't expected to meet much traffic, but there was some. It was mostly long-distance transports, making for Paris in the same direction as ourselves, and the wide dual highway readily absorbed it, while the beech trees, growing close to the verges along the length of the road, smothered the sound. In the car Hugo and I and the dead Sergei were cut off in a small world of our own.

To distract my thoughts, I said: 'You've decided where to go?'

'Yes. About half-way to Waterloo, opposite the road to Hoeilaart, there's a lane into the Forêt, and it widens into a clearing big enough to hold several cars.' Hugo laughed. 'I once saw two buses there disgorging nuns and schoolkids. They were going to have a picnic.'

'Isn't it pretty public?'

'Yes. Which means we can park where scores of other cars park. I know the forest is sixteen or seventeen square miles, Kit, but what with walkers and riders and dogs and lovers you can't guarantee that Sergei won't be found some time. So I'm sure it's best to keep things simple. Let the police form their own theories – if it becomes necessary.'

They weren't encouraging words but there wasn't time to brood on them. Hugo had braked hard. Behind us a truck with a trailer hooted irritably as it passed. Hugo swung the Rover off the road, bumped for perhaps fifty yards along a path and drew up in a clearing; it was as he had described it, except for a small, brick, steep-roofed building, with an iron grille drawn across its open front. As Hugo quickly switched off the car lights candle flames flickered behind the grille.

'What on earth's that?' I said.

'It's called La Chapelle de Notre-Dame de Bonne Odeur, and it's in use. You can't see now, but there's an altar with a plaster statue of the Virgin and jam jars full of flowers. One of these days we might return and light a candle for this poor devil we're about to bury.'

I couldn't tell from Hugo's voice whether he was serious or not. We got out of the car. Under the beech trees it was very dark and, apart from the whisperings of the forest and the soughing of the wind high up in the branches, very still. The traffic on the Route de Mont-Saint-Jean, though so close, was only an undulating murmur.

'Have you got the torch?'

'Yes.'

'Then let's get this over as quickly as we can.'

I shone the pencil light on to the back of the car and Hugo unlocked and opened the boot. Sergei's poor broken body, which had produced such prodigies of dancing with the Bolshoi, looked like a sack of potatoes. But it was far more recalcitrant. Somehow, during the drive from Brussels, it had become wedged under the lip of the opening. And now it would not move.

Hugo and I pulled, pushed, cursed, cajoled. At first we were terrified of doing some unspeakable damage to the corpse. Soon we didn't care. There was the sharp crack of a breaking bone; it was a brutal sound. But the body had come loose.

We carried it past the front of the chapel; the flickering light of the candles inside hardly pierced the darkness. We manœuvred ourselves and our burden around one of the wooden barriers that forbid the *sentiers* and the *pistes* of the Forêt to vehicles, and continued along what in England would be called a bridle-path. In daylight it would have been easy; by night it was almost impossible.

'Hugo, this is hopeless. We can't go on,' I said.

'Put him down. And give me the torch. I won't be a minute.'

It was a very long minute. I could see nothing except small patches of relative light high above me. I could hear the wind exploring the tree tops and other, inexplicable sounds, some of them quite loud. I could feel Sergei's body lying at my feet on the beech nuts, which form a carpet of mast throughout the Fôret. Somewhere an owl hooted and hooted again. I gasped with fright.

'Kit!' Hugo's shape separated itself from a tree.

'Yes.'

'I've found a place. It's really too close to the road and much too close to this path, but it'll have to do.'

We devised a new means of progress. Hugo went first, carrying Sergei in his arms like a baby, and I came behind trying to shine the torch over his shoulder so that he could see where he was going. It was moderately successful but, since the *piste* was very overgrown, it required a tremendous physical effort from Hugo. He was panting with exertion when we reached the place he thought suitable.

'Here – here we are,' he said. 'There's a – a bloody great ditch. I nearly fell in.'

'All right,' I said. 'Let's be quick.'

Sergei's body hit the water at the bottom of the ditch with a sharp splash. I shone the beam of the torch downwards. We could see only the black outline of his leather jacket amongst the green scum and the fern and the detritus. It would be chance if Sergei were found, even when spring came, but I hoped that someone would find him eventually. It might be stupid of me, but I wanted him to have a decent burial. I wasn't cut out for this sort of thing.

Nor was Hugo, in spite of his apparent efficiency. As soon as we returned to the car he fumbled in the glove compartment and produced a flask. He drank before he offered it to me. He hadn't left much, but it was enough. The brandy, the warmth of the car and in a curious fashion the knowledge that what we had done had been unavoidable steadied me. I watched as Hugo put the key into the ignition with a hand that still shook.

We reversed in front of the chapel, which was now in total darkness – either the candles had guttered or the wind had finally blown them out – and drove back to the highway. Hugo put his foot down on the accelerator. The car consumed the kilometres. In no time we were out of the Forêt de Soignes and into the suburbs of Brussels. I was thinking of a hot bath to wash away the physical contact with Sergei's dead body, and bed to wash away all thoughts of it. I felt as if I could sleep for a week. We turned into the entrance to the Residence.

I was startled by the sharpness of Hugo's voice. 'Kit, did you see anything?' Although no one could conceivably have heard us he spoke in little more than a whisper.

'Nothing – nothing peculiar. Did you?'

'As we came round the end of the flower-bed the car lights caught the front of the house. I could have sworn I saw someone climbing in the third or fourth window along.'

'The one that gives on the first-floor corridor?'

'Could be. It happened so quickly. We'd better investigate.' Hugo had stopped the car beside the front door and turned off the engine. 'Let yourself in as if we hadn't noticed a thing. Go upstairs and wake up Simon. Put on all the lights. If anyone gets in your way scream to high heaven. He'll run, I'm sure – unless it's a real burglar this time.'

'What are you going to do?'

'I shall come in the way he did. The creeper wouldn't have held him. There'll either be a ladder or a knotted rope or something.'

'Be careful, Hugo.'

'Of course. But hurry, Kit, or I'll be there before you are.'

As I struggled – all thumbs – to fit my key in the lock I heard an owl hooting in the near-by wood. Usually I liked to hear him, but now he reminded me of his fellow in the Forêt de Soignes. There had been no time to catch my breath between that crisis and this.

I stepped into the hall, switched on the light, and shut the front door. I leant against it, listening, but there were only the usual creakings of the old house. Very quietly I went up the stairs and along the corridor to the rooms occupied by Baranov and, tonight, by Simon. I knocked on their door.

'Who is it?' Simon's voice was thick with sleep.

'It's me. Catherine Rayle.'

The door opened immediately. Simon's sleepiness had been feigned. He was still dressed and in his right hand he held the small, purposeful gun that Hugo had provided. He looked businesslike.

'Hugo thought he saw someone trying to climb into a window on this floor,' I said.

'Another funny burglar?'

'Hugo could have been mistaken.'

'But he could have been right.' Simon came into the corridor and shut and locked the door behind him. 'We shall have to look.'

We didn't have to look far. The draught was apparent before we reached the end of the passage. The window was wide open, the curtains billowing. I shone the torch beam on to the sill. It showed two deep indentations in the woodwork, which might have been caused by the metal grips of a rope ladder. There was no ladder now, and the creeper hung, loose and broken, where it had been torn from the wall. Somebody had climbed through that window not long ago.

'We'll have to wake the servants,' I said. 'Search the whole house. You'd better go back and stay with Baranov.'

Simon, who had leant far over the sill, drew in the upper half of his body. 'There's someone down there,' he said. 'Lying in the drive.'

'Oh God!' I said. 'Hugo!'

We both ran. Regardless of Baranov and any intruders we pounded down the stairs and out of the house. Although he had to open the front door Simon was much quicker than I. He had already picked Hugo up and was helping him to stand when I reached them. Hugo was cursing savagely. I took his other arm, but he pushed me away, and pulled away from Simon.

'For pity's sake!' he said angrily. 'I'm all right.'

'What happened?'

'I was clobbered. I was so busy testing the ladder before I risked my precious life on it that I forgot there'd be another chap watching for the one inside. He came up behind and crowned me.' Hugo felt his head gingerly. 'I don't think the skin's broken, but I'm going to have a hell of a lump in the morning.'

'Let's get back into the house,' I said. 'They'll be searching for Baranov.'

'Damn Baranov!' Hugo said, and added some picturesque details. 'Anyway there's no need to fuss. Our Russian chums have gone.'

'Are you sure?'

'Positive! Apart from the first couple of seconds after he hit me I knew everything that went on. There were two of them, probably a third waiting in a car.' Hugo gestured down the drive in the direction of the road. 'Much the same set-up as – yesterday morning. They could even have been the same men, sent back to finish the job.'

'To kidnap Baranov, you mean?' Simon said.

'Why not? They seem pretty capable characters, and that's the obvious next step.' Hugo's voice was dry. 'If we hadn't turned up as we did, the comrade who climbed in would have dealt with you – '

'How? You make it sound bloody easy,' Simon objected. 'I did have a gun.'

'So what?' said Hugo. 'He was a professional. And you wouldn't have been prepared to shoot. He'd have disarmed you just like that, made you turn round and knocked you out. As for Baranov, a whiff of gas, an injection – anything would have done for him. Then he'd have whistled up the other comrade and off they'd have gone, straight out by the front door probably, with Baranov. They just had bad luck.'

'What do you mean by "whistled-up"?' I said.

'They had walkie-talkies,' Hugo said. 'Another sign of competence. That's why they made such an efficient getaway when we arrived unexpectedly. They must have thought you'd phone for the police, Kit, and rouse the whole household. And the one thing they daren't risk is being caught and identified as Soviet citizens. It's only because they're scared of a diplomatic incident that we've got away with all we have.'

'Poor old Baranov,' Simon said, half under his breath. 'He'd have woken up in the Russian Embassy and God knows what they'd have done to him.'

'That could still happen, unless we do something about it,' Hugo said. 'Poor old Baranov could go back to his Russian chums. And all those lovely little secrets that he promised to give to NATO could go with him. Or has he confided them to you, Kit?'

'No. Why should he? I haven't asked him and he didn't volunteer,' I said, irritated by Hugo's sudden inconsequence. 'Let's go inside.'

We were standing by the front door now and the light from the hall streamed out towards the oval-shaped flower-bed. I could see Hugo's face clearly. His sardonic grin was growing wider. 'My dear Kit,' he said. He put his arm round my shoulder, pretending to lean on me as we went into the house. He was shaking with humourless laughter.

'My dear Kit,' he said again. 'I should ask him, if I were you – certainly before you present him to the Secretary General. I'll bet you – anything you like – you'll have a shock.'

Chapter 12

I had a few hours' essential sleep before going to the office – late. As always I found my desk weighed down with work of no real importance. The final draft of my speech for the Atlantic Assembly, now neatly typed, sat in the centre of my blotting pad, and there was a pile of telegrams, documents, minutes, of which perhaps fifteen per cent would need some action; I had no enthusiasm for any of it. To one side were the English newspapers. I picked up *The Times*.

Simon was at the Residence, watching over Baranov, but somebody had thought to mark the papers for my attention. On the foreign news page of *The Times* – the story had already been relegated to the inside of the paper – I found a half-column, side-lined in red, about the incident at the Vienna Opera House.

It was clear who had come off worst. Of the seven dead, one was the stage manager, one a member of the riot squad, and the remaining five were 'Fighters for Free Austria'. Several people were in hospital suffering from smoke inhalation, but none were in serious condition, and there had been surprisingly little damage to the Opera House itself. The remaining three 'Fighters' had been captured and could look forward to long prison sentences. By prompt and, some would be bound to say, brutal action, the defenders of law and order had triumphed.

I glanced at the rest of the papers. Depending on their political bias they told the story in different ways, but they added nothing new. Only the writer of the third leader in the *Daily Telegraph* mentioned the general unrest in Austria and the possibility of what he chose to call 'communist-inspired happenings during the run-up to the coming elections'. I was wondering exactly what he had left unstated when the buzzing of the intercom interrupted me, and immediately afterwards the secure telephone rang.

My secretary said: 'Lady Rayle, I have a Mademoiselle Louise Fromberg on the line.'

'I can't talk now,' I said and, into the red telephone: 'Hullo, this is Catherine Rayle speaking.'

'Good morning, Lady Rayle. This is Sir Richard Tindle's deputy.'

'She says it's very urgent and she has already called –'

I flicked the switch to cut off the intercom. I had never heard of Louise Fromberg. 'Good morning,' I said. 'I was about to telephone you. I should have done before, but I've been – occupied. I assume Sir Richard's abroad, as usual, or at any rate too busy to talk to me himself?'

There was a lengthening silence and I imagined him casting his eyes to heaven in a prayer for patience. He ignored my question. 'I telephone for two reasons,' he said. 'The first is Sergei Alexandrov. I regret we've not been able –'

'He was delivered to me yesterday evening, but so badly damaged that Hugo Pewter and I had to throw him away – in the Forêt de Soignes.'

'What!'

'It was not a pleasant thing to do, but there was no alternative. He was – was beyond repair when he was left at the Residence. If there'd been any hope –'

'I – I understand, Lady Rayle.' He had recovered quickly. 'But the other parcel, that's still all right?'

'Yes – just.'

He asked me more about Sergei and, when I had satisfied him, I went on to describe Baranov's failure to get away on Sunday night and the Russians' two possible attempts to repossess him. Meanwhile I doodled on my memo pad, making a pretty pattern over the list of people who had, or hoped to have, appointments with me later in the day. At the bottom of my list my secretary had written: 'Mlle Louise Fromberg, Hôtel Dieu, phoned twice – urgent.' And part of my brain registered that after all I did know the persistent Miss Fromberg; she was the Flemish nurse in charge of the man who had turned out not to be Sergei. Carefully I extended the doodle so that it obliterated her name. I was sorry about her concussed Englishman, but he wasn't my problem and he could become a nuisance.

'. . . Secretary General will be back tomorrow and I've made an appointment to see him.'

'Which doesn't leave the opposition much time.'

'But enough.'

'Yes. Well – my second reason for telephoning you, Lady Rayle, was to tell you that Sir Richard hopes to arrive in Brussels today. He'll get in touch with you as soon as possible and arrange a meeting.'

He was irritatingly vague about the when, where and how of Dick's movements. I replaced the receiver with a bang. I had my customary feeling of having been moved around a chess-board. And I did not like being a pawn. Yet, I had to admit, on the few occasions I was allowed to be a queen I had to run hard to stay in the same place.

I called in my secretary and told her to cancel my engagements for the evening – cocktails with the Dutch Permrep and dinner with the German Ambassador, one of whose flaxen-haired daughters would be happy to take my place at table. If Mademoiselle Fromberg phoned again, she was to be told I was not available. I wanted to see the Minister at his convenience. Then I got down to the paper chores.

It was almost twelve-thirty when Hugo appeared. He had spent the morning at a Political Advisers meeting and was not in the best of tempers. He showed no surprise at the news that Dick Tindle would be arriving.

'He's coming himself, is he? I thought he might.'

'Why?'

'My dear Kit, you can't hide Baranov for much longer and the NATO Council aren't really interested in ballet.'

'What's that supposed to mean?'

'You haven't asked Baranov about this invaluable information he's so keen to give to the Secretary General, have you?'

'No. There hasn't been time since you suggested I should.'

'If you had, you'd have discovered he hasn't got any information, invaluable or otherwise, to offer anybody.' Hugo grinned at my blank face. 'I warned you that you were in for a shock, Kit.'

'Are you saying that this is some other trick of Marika's.'

'Not according to Baranov. I had a private audience with him yesterday. I insisted, in spite of Simon's disapproval. Baranov says he's waiting for the British to provide whatever it is he's to pass on to NATO. And that, I suspect, is exactly why Dick Tindle's appearing on the scene.'

'The whole thing's like an onion,' I said angrily, 'layer on layer, and none of it makes sense.'

Hugo laughed. 'Go and powder Your Excellency's nose and I'll take you to lunch,' he said. 'We have to eat.'

The buzzer sounded. Sir Thomas Bright wished to speak to me. He was always polite but on the telephone he tended to be abrupt. Today he was curt. With the minimum of *plaisanteries* he invited me to cocktails at seven – an unexpected party for an old friend who had descended on him – and with the minimum of thought I refused. My attention was on Hugo who had found the camera he had lent me. I had brought it to the office to return to him, and he was miming that he would take it. I was nodding and pointing at the envelope containing the Polaroid prints of the long man in the hospital bed – the man who was certainly no ballet dancer.

'Catherine!'

Somehow, in that one word, Tommy Bright managed to suggest an excess of vinegar in a salad dressing. He coughed, cleared his throat and apologized. Simultaneously I realized the reason for this sudden invitation, and why Tommy disliked it so much. He must have had instructions from London.

'Mayn't I persuade you to reconsider, Catherine? We should so like to see you – and the Minister too. Perhaps you'd be kind enough to give Hugo the message.'

I put down the receiver slowly, thinking that tonight's plans for protecting Baranov would have to be changed but that once Dick was here the responsibility would be his. 'Seven o'clock, cocktails at the Brights. Both of us,' I said to Hugo. 'It would have been more convenient if Dick had come straight to the Residence.'

Hugo grunted. He had taken the prints to the window. I left him to it. When I came back from the cloakroom, ready to go out to lunch, he was sitting at my desk, peering at them through a magnifying glass.

'If only he didn't have that damned bandage round his head,' Hugo said, to himself rather than to me.

'Don't tell me you recognize him?'

'I've seen him, or his first cousin, somewhere, and in the last year.'

'Oh, for God's sake!'

My exclamation covered both my disbelief in Hugo's claim, and the intercom buzzer. But the latter was only a call from Simon to report that everything at the Residence remained peaceful.

'All right,' Hugo said. 'Let's go.'

We went, in Hugo's car. Rule had driven me to the office in the Rolls as usual, but he was now standing guard at the Residence. Simon had to have some support and I had been prepared to trust Rule enough to ask him to keep his eyes skinned for any more potential burglars. It turned out he used a rifle for potting rabbits and, armed with this, he was patrolling the grounds under the guise of casual gardening. What with Simon's gun and Rule's rifle the Residence seemed to be steadily degenerating into an armed camp.

Hugo took me to a small restaurant in the Ilót Sacré where, though the place was full, a corner table materialized at his request. I think it had been added especially for him for we were very close to our neighbours, which was a good thing; it meant we couldn't talk about our problems. By the time we had finished an aperitif – a speciality of the house made of champagne, brandy and peach juice – I had begun to unwind. The food that followed was excellent, the wine pleasant, and I was actually enjoying myself when, in the middle of a sentence, Hugo's voice tailed away. He sat, staring at the lettuce twisted round his fork as if he weren't sure that it was good to eat. Slowly he put it in his mouth and began to chew. Then he played with the salad on his plate.

My patience gave out. 'Hugo, what's the matter?'

'I last saw Dick Tindle when my masters summoned me to London to tell me you were going to be the new Permrep,' he said carefully. 'I was lunching at the Savoy Grill, trying to get over the shock, when Tindle came in. There was another chap with him, quite a bit younger, tall, red-haired, grey-eyed, craggy-faced.'

'And you think – '

'That as soon as we've had coffee, which I insist on, we'd better pay a call on this character at the Hôtel Dieu.'

It wasn't as simple as one might have thought. By the time we reached the hospital visiting hours had begun. The place was teeming with flower-bearing friends and relations, all eager to get to the bedsides of their sick. There was nowhere to park, and a queue at the enquiry desk.

We decided to find the room for ourselves. Nobody tried to stop us. Nobody helped us either, even when we got slightly lost. The staff were too preoccupied. Something seemed to be wrong. There was a lot of coming and going everywhere, unconnected with the visitors, and an air of suppressed excitement. Nurses and orderlies whispered in corners. Doctors strode past, looking grim. For some reason the normal working of the hospital had been disturbed.

We found the room eventually. The door was half open and, after a gentle tap, we went in. The first thing I saw was the bed, neatly made, flat, empty; no water or fruit juice on the side table, no medicines. But by the window was a great bowl of chrysanthemums, the flowers I had collected from La Marguerite, the flowers that Nurse Fromberg had arranged for *le pauvre*.

Hugo frowned. 'Could he have been discharged?'

'Not unless someone claimed him. And he can't have died,' I said, thrusting away the thought. 'He was a sick man but not – not in any danger.'

'Then he must have been moved to another room,' Hugo said with assurance.

'Who are you? What are you doing in here?' a voice said in French. 'Oh, it's you, Lady Rayle. You've come after all – when it's too late.'

Mademoiselle Fromberg had been crying; her eyes were

bloodshot and watery, her cheeks blotched. But she was angry, too. She gave a loud sniff.

'Why wouldn't you speak to me on the telephone, Lady Rayle?'

'Never mind about the phone, Mademoiselle,' Hugo said gently. 'We're here now, so come and sit down and tell us what's happened to your patient.'

'You don't understand,' she said, but she took the chair that Hugo drew up for her, and managed a tearful smile in his direction. 'You're not from the police, are you, Monsieur?'

'Me – from the police?' Hugo shook his head. 'No. I'm from the British Embassy. You can trust me, I assure you, Mademoiselle.'

'Monsieur Pewter thinks he may have met your patient,' I said.

'You know him? You know Monsieur Robinson? But –' The light faded from her face. She sighed. 'It's too late, Monsieur. He's no longer at the hospital. If only you had answered the telephone, Lady Rayle, sent him some message . . .'

'I was here yesterday afternoon,' I protested.

'It was after you left that he remembered. I helped him to remember and he said he could – could kiss me.' Tears filled her eyes again. She produced a damp handkerchief from a pocket under her apron and blew her nose aggressively. 'He kept on muttering, "Catherine", "Catherine", so I showed him the card which came with the flowers you brought him and he said that was it, you were Catherine Rayle, Lady Rayle. And after a while he remembered other things, like his name, Jim Robinson, but he made me promise I wouldn't tell anybody except you. I was to phone you at NATO Headquarters. I was to say he was a friend of Dick, from London, and he must speak with you, *at once*. But I couldn't give you the message. I tried. The good God knows how I tried. When I came on duty at noon I told Monsieur Robinson and he said he understood.' She gave me a baleful glance and stopped, as if she had come to the end of her story.

'And later, perhaps when you brought his lunch,' Hugo prompted, 'he had disappeared?'

'Yes – and his clothes from the closet. But he's a sick man, Monsieur. He can't have gone far by himself, and he has no money, no friends. Yet he's not in the hospital. We have searched everywhere. And now Matron has set the police on him. She's very angry. She says this sort of thing is bad for our reputation. And everyone is upset.'

Giving Mademoiselle Fromberg all kinds of false promises, we got out of the Hôtel Dieu as fast as we could. It was imperative that we should find the man who called himself Jim Robinson before he was caught by the police, or collapsed in the street. He was almost certainly the man that Dick's other friend had called the Captain. What he had to tell us could be vital.

'Where do you think he'll make for?' I said as we hurried towards the car park.

'The Residence,' Hugo said, 'without a doubt. If he can get there he'll expect to be safe and taken care of and that someone'll find you for him. He won't know the house is guarded like a fortress with Rule and his rifle.'

'And if Rule won't let him in and shoos him away as a suspicious character, what then – NATO HQ?'

'That's the next most likely place, I imagine. But we don't want him making a scene there, or giving messages when he's half-conscious to someone like David Driscole.'

'What about telephoning the Residence?'

I had to shout. As soon as we got in the car Hugo had leaned on the horn. He continued to lean on it until the parking attendant came to move a small Toyota out of the way. He shook his head to my question, however, and mouthed: 'Quicker to go,' which was a moot point. We had scraped past the Toyota when another small car blocked us.

'Why the hell don't you learn to drive?' Hugo demanded.

'It's no use swearing at them in English,' I said. 'They won't understand.'

'It relieves my feelings, and anyway they don't understand French either, not those *types*.'

To prove him right we got some return abuse in Flemish. And, as we edged into the road, scattering a bunch of pedestrians just unloaded from a bus, a woman angrily threatened us with the flowers she was carrying. I didn't blame her. Hugo drove fiercely through the winding streets and on to the boulevards, where we overtook car after car. We were at the Residence sooner than I would have believed possible.

The large house sprawled in the wintry sunshine, the windows all closed, most of them on the ground floor shuttered. Except for a wisp of smoke from the chimneys it could have been deserted. There was no sign of Rule.

I rang the doorbell, giving the prearranged signal, and after what seemed a long pause we heard the bolts being drawn. Even then, since they were stiff from lack of use it was another minute before the houseman let us into the hall. Everything was well, he assured us. Nobody had called except people known to him and nobody, on any pretext, had sought to enter the house. Mr Maryton was feeling better; he had eaten a large lunch. Rule? No, he had not seen Rule for some while.

I left Hugo to telephone the office and went upstairs to check on Simon and Baranov. They were lazing away the day, playing records, being bored, yearning for exercise. Nothing had happened; nothing, Baranov implied nastily, was ever going to happen again.

'Tomorrow,' I promised him, 'when the Secretary General returns.' And to Simon, who had followed me to the door, I added in what I hoped was an encouraging whisper: 'Dick Tindle will be here this evening.'

I went downstairs and along to my study, where I assumed Hugo would be telephoning. I was halfway into the room, shutting the door behind me, before I took in the situation. For a moment I stared. Then I collapsed into the nearest chair and laughed. Not one of the three men managed a smile.

Hugo, his face devoid of any emotion, stood with his back against the wall. He had taken off his overcoat and his jacket, which were lying on the floor some distance from him. His hands hovered on his hips and it was clear, from Rule's appearance, what Hugo was about to do. Rule, red-faced and angry, stood close by. His hands were clasped behind his neck and his trousers were around his ankles; he was sporting yellow underpants with bright green dragons on them. I wasn't to know what Hugo was wearing. Deliberately he hitched up the trousers he had been about to drop and zipped up the fly.

'Your Excellency,' he said, somehow managing not to sound pompous, 'would you please tell this madman who we are.'

'Give that rifle back to my chauffeur, Mr Robinson – or whatever you call yourself,' I said. I no longer wanted to laugh. 'The police are looking for you and the hospital's anxious about you, but you're quite safe here.'

'Lady Rayle!' The slate-grey eyes glittered in the craggy face. 'I struggled into my clothes, I stole some money for a taxi, I walked out of that hospital where by rights I ought to be – because I need to see you. I have to speak to you, alone.'

'Don't be so bloody melodramatic,' Hugo said.

It took about five minute to sort things out, to explain Hugo, to assuage Rule's pride, to order soup and sandwiches and coffee for Mr Robinson. He was looking a dirty white, and there were beads of perspiration on his forehead; I was afraid he might faint, but he was going to tell me – and against his will, Hugo – what he had come to say.

'My job was to collect a parcel and deliver it in good working order to you, Lady Rayle,' he began. 'Anna de Lisle contacted me, the time and place of delivery were arranged but, unfortunately, the collection arrangements included a car accident, and during the accident I was rather badly hurt. My Number Two was already ill. I was dependent on a muscle man and another chap, who really did damn well to look after me and – and the parcel, which had also got damaged.'

He stopped. He must have been very sensitive to atmosphere. Hugo and I had both reacted to his assessment of events.

'If you want to ask any questions, please do,' he said. 'Or tell me if what I'm saying is out-dated. You must remember that up to yesterday evening I've only had periods of lucidity. I've not read the newspapers or heard a radio.'

'No questions,' Hugo said. 'But let's stop talking about parcels, shall we? This room isn't bugged, and it's confusing.'

'Very well.' He held his head between his hands for a moment as if it were paining him. 'Because Baranov and I were both hurt everything was delayed. But how much delayed? That's what I must know. They promised to deliver him here. Did they? Where is he now?'

I waited for Hugo to have the pleasure of telling Mr Robinson that he had seized the wrong dancer from the Russians, and that we had had to rescue Baranov ourselves, but Hugo only said: 'He's upstairs.'

'Thank God for that,' he said. 'Then I'm not too late.'

'Too late for what?'

'To brief him properly before you take him to the Secretary General, Lady Rayle. I did have a go. I made my chaps leave me alone with him and I tried – but it can't have been much good. And I was afraid neither you nor he would realize that he wasn't fully prepared, and you'd go ahead, and the whole op would be nullified.'

He broke off as there was a knock on the door. The houseman came in with a tray of food. I told him that Mr Robinson would be staying the night, and which room to get ready, and he bowed himself out.

'In fact, Baranov's not briefed at all,' Hugo said as if there had been no interruption. 'He knows that he has to take his information to the Secretary General and that his quotable source is his girl-friend, Marika, but he doesn't know about – ' He paused, cleared his throat, coughed. 'About – ' He had a fit of coughing.

'You were saying?' Mr Robinson said, not falling into the trap of completing Hugo's sentence.

'Baranov doesn't know about – the essential details,' Hugo said calmly.

Mr Robinson finished his soup and ate a sandwich without speaking. He didn't seem very hungry. Once, for several seconds, he shut his eyes. He wasn't far from collapse.

'I'll introduce you to Baranov later this evening,' I said, 'but now you must rest. This briefing won't take very long, will it?'

'No time at all, when we're both in our right minds.' He gave me a brilliant smile. 'Baranov doesn't have to memorize "the essential details". They're all on a piece of ultrafiche that Dick put in the watch. He just has to explain how Marika's supposed to have got hold of it, and why she gave it to him. It's not too difficult.'

Hugo was frowning. 'You mean that this isn't genuine Soviet intelligence?' he said slowly. 'Tindle's trying to get NATO to accept some fake information?'

'Like hell I do! The info's genuine all right – straight from the Kremlin. Chaps have died to get it to us.' Mr Robinson sounded angry. 'But no one in the West will believe it – they won't want to – unless Baranov substantiates it, provides the provenance as it were.' His eyes shut again and he swayed slightly. 'And God help us all if they don't.'

'Well, you can give him the watch and brief him later – '

'He has the watch, Lady Rayle. At least I made sure of that. The first thing I did after the car crash was to – to slip it on his – his wrist.' Mr Robinson rocked his head gently from side to side. 'Oh God! Sorry! I – I feel . . . better soon.'

We caught him as he pitched forward and managed to settle him back in the corner of his big chair, a cushion behind his head. His breathing was heavy but regular. Over his recumbent body Hugo and I looked at each other.

'Kit, you – you heard what he said?'

'Yes. The really vital thing is a bit of ultrafiche – that's some form of microfilm, isn't it? It was hidden in a watch, which Robinson's positive he put on Baranov's wrist. That can only mean he put it on – on Sergei.'

And Sergei Alexandrov was lying in a ditch in the Forêt de Soignes, where Hugo and I had thrown him in the early hours of this morning. Someone would have to go back and . . .

Even the thought of it was revolting.

Chapter 13

As a child I had a recurrent nightmare. The unpleasant sensations resulting from it used to linger long after I was awake. They were indefinable and I hadn't experienced them for years. Now, however, when Hugo turned the car on to the Route de Mont-Saint-Jean for the second time in less than twenty-four hours, I recognized them again. They were horrible.

'Cold?'

'No.' I shivered. 'Just nerves.'

'It's all my fault. To think I searched Sergei in case Dick's bloody friend had left a message in his clothes and never looked at his watch!' Disgusted with himself, Hugo hooted viciously at a lorry that had cut in too sharply in front of us. 'To be honest, Kit, I don't even remember him having a watch.'

I didn't answer. I stared out of the car window at the great beech trees rushing past. It was early evening but already dark and, after a fine day, beginning to spit with rain. The swish of the windshield wipers was irritating. Hugo turned on the radio and for a moment we were drowned in pop music. Impatiently he tried other stations, then switched off.

'By the way, Kit, Daphne'll be coming with us to the Brights'.'

'Daphne?' I kept my voice neutral. 'You don't think Dick will object?'

'Why the hell should he? It's a party. Why shouldn't I bring her? We were going to play bridge with the Richardsons – the US Counsellor and his wife – and some other people. But since I can't make it and Daphne doesn't want to go alone, the obvious thing is for her to come to the Brights' party too.'

'What have you told her – about what's been happening?'

'Nothing. Why do you ask?'

'I thought she'd have wanted to know where you were and

what you were doing in the evenings.'

'I – I said there was a minor crisis at the office. She's used to me having to do duty at odd times. Besides – ' Hugo shrugged – 'she doesn't keep track of all my movements. Daphne's an understanding woman, Kit. If she were one of those possessive wives she wouldn't have put up with me for so long.'

Hugo, concentrating on the road, luckily didn't see the amazement stamped on my face. Daphne was the last person I would have called understanding and, as for not being a possessive wife, I considered her the epitome of possessiveness. Nor was I the only one. I remembered hearing someone say that Daphne Pewter had never had a child because she refused to stand the competition. It was a hideously unkind remark, of course, but there could have been some truth in it. I wondered if Hugo really believed what he had said.

We turned off the highway and drove in among the trees. The little parking space beside La Chapelle de Notre Dame de Bonne Odeur was as deserted as it had been in the small hours. But someone had been there since we had: there were fresh candles burning behind the iron grille. I should never know who lit them or why, but they made me feel nervous. Reluctantly I got out of the car.

'Please God we'll be able to find the ditch again,' Hugo said, unlocking the boot.

He had come prepared. We had brought gumboots in case we had to wade in the ditch to pull up Sergei's body. We had brought gauntlets in the hope that we wouldn't have to touch his flesh. We had brought a hook – the sort of thing you see in a butcher's window with a carcase hanging on it. Simon had unearthed the hook from somewhere in the Residence and suggested it might be useful. Nobody had been specific as to exactly what we might do with it. We had brought a powerful torch. Apart from the torch everything was in a canvas hold-all.

It was as dark in the Forêt de Soignes as it had been during the previous night, but even quieter. There was no wind and the rain wasn't heavy enough to beat on the leaves. Everything seemed asleep, except for an almost inaudible whispering. Hugo and I, though we were walking on a flooring of mast and spoke very little, made a disproportionate disturbance.

We had no trouble finding the right *sentier*, but it wasn't so easy to locate the right *piste*. We ignored several that branched off our path, only to have to retrace our steps when we realized that we had come too far and missed the one we wanted.

'I suppose we'll have to try them all,' Hugo said bitterly.

In fact we were lucky the second time – if lucky isn't an inapposite word in such circumstances. Hugo, who was shining the torch ahead, stopped so abruptly that I ran into him. He turned and caught me.

'Don't look!'

But I had already looked and seen. Burying my head in Hugo's shoulder, I stifled a scream. For a moment we clung to each other. We were both shaking.

'The watch! Hugo, we've got to get it. We must.'

The effort required to look once more at that ghastly sight was tremendous, but, since it was no longer unexpected, it had lost something of its horror. We had left Sergei a black, huddled form at the bottom of the ditch. We found him seemingly half crouched upon the bank as if, driven back by someone or something, he had failed at the last gasp to climb out of his grave.

There was a simple explanation. Around dawn, when the high wind had subsided, a heavy fall of rain must have caused a flash flood in the ditch. Sergei's body had then floated, or been pushed to the surface by the build-up of detritus. And some animal, a rat perhaps, smelling it out, had gnawed the flesh disgustingly.

'The hook,' I said, trying not to choke over the words. 'We – we won't have to touch him, Hugo.'

Hugo opened the hold-all and brought out the hook while I shone the light for him. We had to hurry; if we were slow or stopped to think what we were doing, our nerve would go. But Hugo's fumblings seemed to take forever, and my patience snapped. I swore at him.

He glared at me, seized my hand and pointed the beam of the torch that I was holding directly at Sergei. Then he thrust the hook under Sergei's shoulder and pulled. The body came out of the ditch fast. Hugo and I recoiled, knocking against each other. I dropped the torch. The light flickered, but it did not go out, which was absurdly, illogically heartening.

I snatched up the torch and focused it on Sergei again. He was lying on his left side. The sleeve of his jacket was rucked up so that the wrist and lower part of his right arm were visible. They were, as one would have expected, bare.

Hugo seized the butcher's hook, which had torn away from Sergei's shoulder when we staggered back from the edge of the ditch, and brutally turned the body over. Time was running out. My stomach was cramping and the bile was rising in my throat. Hugo dropped the hook and with his gloved hands pushed up the left sleeve. On his wrist Sergei was wearing a gold bracelet.

There was no watch.

Hugo and I didn't speak. We acted together. Savagely he kicked Sergei back into the ditch and in one movement scooped up the hook and the hold-all. We ran. I tried to hold the torch so that it illuminated the *piste* ahead of us but the light wobbled from side to side. I went straight into a tree. I fell to my knees, and vomited my heart out. Not far from me Hugo too was being sick.

'My dear old Kit, are you all right?'

Hugo was beside me, helping me to my feet, rubbing my hump hard, so that he hurt as well as warmed me. I wiped my face on the handkerchief he offered. There was a vile taste in my mouth.

'Let's get out of here – back to the car.'

'Yes. Thanks be, I remembered to refill the flask.'

We sat in the Rover, sipping brandy and waiting for our stomachs to settle. From time to time, although the heater was on and there was a good fug in the car, one or other of us shivered. Gradually, however, we recovered our composure.

'What the hell could have happened to that watch, Kit? Robinson was positive he'd put it on Baranov's wrist. For Baranov, read Sergei, of course.'

'It's certainly not there now. Perhaps one of Robinson's men took it as a souvenir, without realizing its importance.'

'In that case – and it's a possibility, I suppose – God knows what happens. There doesn't seem much point in Baranov trying to authenticate a bit of ultrafiche, however important, if he hasn't got it.' Suddenly Hugo put his arm around my shoulders and hugged me. 'Dearest Kit, we'd better go and break the news to our Dick.'

Hugo dropped me at the Residence. The place was ablaze with light and already there were three or four cars parked in the drive. Simon was about to give a party. On the pretext of celebrating his return to health he had telephoned some of his friends and invited them in for drinks and a buffet supper.

It had been Hugo's suggestion. He had been fairly sure that as long as there were a lot of comings and goings, signs of activity and bright lights, the Russians wouldn't dare to make another attack on Baranov. A party, therefore, might prove a more effective defence of the Residence than Rule and his rifle had been, and shorten the number of hours in which we were vulnerable.

The front door opened before I had my key in the lock. Simon had been waiting for me. A smile quivered on his mouth but didn't reach his eyes. He said, far too brightly:

'Hullo, Lady Rayle. I saw you from the window. We're planning to turn up the rug in the drawing-room later so that we can dance. I hope you don't mind?'

'Not a bit. I've just come back to change. The Minister and Mrs Pewter are picking me up in half an hour.'

We sounded like a couple of would-be RADA students trying out for a poor play. But we had given some of Simon's newly-arrived guests a chance to drift tactfully from the hall. I looked my question.

'Lady Rayle, something extraordinary has happened.'

'Baranov?'

'No. He's all right. In fact, he's in very good form. Our Mr Robinson's impressed him greatly; he's managed to convince him that he'll soon be with his Marika.'

'What is it, then?'

But Simon seemed reluctant to talk in the hall and, though I would have loved to let it go, I knew I couldn't. Heaving a sigh, I led the way to my study.

'Simon, I haven't much time.'

He nodded and began to speak very rapidly. 'Lady Rayle, this afternoon, after I'd told Baranov about Mr Robinson he got very excited and – and to humour him I said I'd find him a small suitcase so that he could pack the few things he has. Most of my luggage is rather good and I didn't want to give him any of it, so I decided to empty the old fibre case where I'd stored his gear. I mean the gear he wore as Albrecht. You remember you said I –'

'I remember.'

My patience was wearing thin. I was listening to Simon with only half my attention. This was mainly because my stomach was beginning to knot again. Soon I would want to be sick. I tried not to think of Sergei, his face part eaten . . . I shut my eyes.

'Lady Rayle, you're not well.'

Simon had startled me. 'Sorry. We had a – a bad time in the Forêt. And there was no watch.'

'No watch!' He stared at me in disbelief. 'Oh God! What'll we do?'

'I don't know yet. Get on with what you were saying.'

'Lady Rayle, the tights that Baranov wore as Albrecht. They were with everything else in the fibre suitcase under the bed. They've disappeared. Somebody must have taken them.'

'But why on earth should anyone –'

'I'm terribly sorry. If only I hadn't asked him to give them to me! It's my fault.'

'Nonsense!'

'They were there yesterday afternoon. I showed the whole costume to Hugo. But that's not much help, is it?' He shook his head in disgust.

In effect, it reduced the list of suspects to the Residence staff and the hundred-odd guests who had attended my reception for the DCDS. Of these the houseman and his wife would have had the most opportunity, but that was no justification for accusing them. I sighed. It was an insoluble problem and, as I told Simon, I didn't see that there was anything to be done about it.

My stomach suddenly contracted and I fled upstairs. In the comfort of my own bathroom I rid myself of some black bile, swilled out my mouth and felt better. I hurried to shower, to dry my hair, to change my clothes from the skin up. Time was short and I would have to see Mr Robinson and tell him about the watch before I left for the Embassy. But Hugo and Daphne, and Dick Tindle could wait. I hadn't actually touched Sergei. Nevertheless, I desperately needed to wash away the memory of those minutes in the Forêt de Soignes.

The Brights' party was being held in one of the large reception rooms at the Embassy. Glancing around while the major-domo waited to announce me, I didn't recognize any of the guests, but I noticed that they all seemed to know each other. From this, and the fact that there were many more men than women, I deduced that they must be delegates to some conference, whom the Ambassador felt obliged to entertain. Dick Tindle, as far as I could see, was not among them.

'Catherine, how very kind of you to come.'

'Not at all. It's a great pleasure, Tommy.'

'Have you heard the latest news from Vienna?' He leaned towards me. 'The Austrians are cracking down on their left wing. There are to be all sorts of new restrictions. That Opera House business really scared them.'

'Splendid.'

'That's what I said, my dear,' Lady Bright greeted me. 'But Tommy's not so sure. He's inclined to think that everybody's reacting too violently.'

I passed perfunctorily down the line. Following behind me Daphne was explaining in her piping, little girl's voice that Rule, my chauffeur, was sick and so we had all come together. I heard Lady Bright mention Simon, something about his having recovered. Tommy and Hugo had their heads together and were obviously talking shop.

'Lady Rayle?'

He was an attractive young man, intelligent, well-groomed, self-assured. Though he wouldn't have been flattered, he reminded me of one of my more elegant students.

'H.E. asked me to look after you, Lady Rayle.' He gave me a slight bow, which underlined the resemblance. 'May I suggest some champagne and perhaps five minutes with the guests – not more, we're running late – before we – er – move along?'

He produced champagne and introduced me to a small group of people, who immediately asked me if there wasn't something I could do to outlaw all nuclear tests, above and below ground. Suppressing a strong desire to inform them that I was part of NATO, not the United Nations, I realized who they were – a collection of environmentalists, concerned with the Committee on the Challenges of Modern Society.

The young man had reappeared with Hugo. He led us casually across the room as if to introduce us to someone, but instead took us through a side door and along a passage. He knocked, waited for the door to be opened, and announced us.

'Catherine, my dear.'

Dick Tindle came forward with both hands outstretched. He kissed me on the cheek and held me at arms' length. He looked tired, I thought, older than when we had last met, and unkempt. There were pouches under his eyes, his hair was lank and needed cutting, his skin had a jaundiced tinge. He looked rather as I felt.

Behind us Hugo gave a dry cough. 'Good evening, Dick.'

'Evening, Hugo. You're late, I regret to say, and my time's short.'

'We've been in the Forêt de Soignes,' Hugo said coldly. 'We were led to suppose that the corpse of one Sergei Alexandrov, a Russian ballet dancer whom we tossed into a ditch last night, was wearing a watch containing a piece of ultra-important ultra-fiche that you want Baranov to authenticate. Our information proved incorrect. The watch was missing – and so is the ultra-fiche! And we've no idea where it might be.'

It was obviously a most bitter blow. Dick went white around the mouth, his lips set in a thin line and his nostrils pinched. Otherwise his face was devoid of expression. He frightened me. I thought he might faint.

'May we help ourselves?' Hugo asked, gesturing towards the bottles on a side table.

'Be the taxpayers' guest,' Dick said evenly.

Hugo opened a bottle of champagne, deliberately making the cork pop and letting the wine froth. He poured a glass for me and one for himself. Dick watched him, saying nothing, thinking, sipping his whisky. He waited for Hugo to sit down.

'You seem to expect apologies – explanations,' he said, addressing Hugo. 'At the moment I don't propose to offer you either. I want to know what the present situation is.'

'Baranov is at the Residence,' I said. 'He's safe, well and, because of Marika, co-operative. Your Mr Robinson is with him now, briefing him for his meeting with the Secretary General tomorrow, if there's any point in going ahead without the – '

'Mr Robinson?'

'Big, craggy gent with red hair and violent habits,' Hugo said.

'Iain!' Dick's tired face lit up with pleasure and relief. 'Thank God for that. I've been looking for him everywhere. Where the devil's he been?'

'In hospital,' I said.

'Hospital?'

'Yes. There was a car accident. He was badly hurt. He practically went through the windscreen. He's been suffering from concussion and – '

'You mean he's been out of action? But – how long?'

I began to explain and Hugo cut me short. 'Your precious Iain's the one who mucked things up,' he said to Dick. 'He grabbed Sergei from the Russians' car instead of Baranov. He briefed Sergei believing he was Baranov. He slipped the damned watch on Sergei's wrist, not Baranov's and it's not there any more. So what, may I ask, are you going to do about it?'

Dick shook his head. 'I was depending on Iain,' he said, 'absolutely. He had complete charge of the Brussels end. God in heaven, who could have guessed he'd get himself knocked out? What a mess! What a mess!' Suddenly he seemed to recollect himself.

'As to what to do, there's really no choice. The ultrafiche is irreplaceable of course, and so is the Baranov-Marika set-up. What's more time's getting short. We'll have to use what we've got. Baranov will have to convince the Secretary General and the Council without the ultrafiche.' He got up and poured himself another whisky. 'Does Iain know it's lost?'

'Yes,' I said. 'I told him just before I came here.'

'Good.' Dick nodded. 'Then he'll have been giving the problem some thought. I'll ask you to take a note to him, Catherine.' He smiled at me. 'Don't worry. Iain will cope – if anyone can.'

'Yes, I'm sure, but – don't forget, Dick – he's not a well man.'

'He'll be all right. He doesn't have to do anything active.' Impatience made his voice harsh and I couldn't press the point. 'Now, there are a couple of things I want to know. The first is, if Iain's people mistook Sergei for Baranov, what happened to Baranov? How did he get to the Residence?'

Hugo told him, somewhat curtly, not stressing the importance of what he himself had done. When he finished Dick looked at me reproachfully.

'Catherine, why didn't you report this? Didn't you see how crucial it could be? You let us think Iain's people had taken Sergei in addition to Baranov, not instead of him.'

I hesitated. I hadn't intended to give such an impression. The truth was that I hadn't bothered to tell Dick's unsympathetic deputy the whole story, and what I had said had been misinterpreted. Hugo saved me from explanations.

'What's your other question?'

'Has either of you any idea how the Russians found out where Baranov was?'

'None,' Hugo said. 'I've given it some thought and discussed it with Simon – and Kit, but no answer. Anyway, it's academic now, surely?'

'Maybe.' Dick seemed to brood about it for a moment. Then he got to his feet. 'Hugo, if you'll excuse us . . . There are one or two things I'd like to discuss with Catherine.'

Hugo stared at him. 'You mean that after killing a KGB man, playing around with a corpse, being hit on the head by a Russian and God knows what else, I'm out – just like that? You're not even going to have the decency to tell me what it's all been in aid of?'

'You have no need to know, Hugo. You know too much already. Remember, tomorrow you have to be as surprised and horrified as anyone that Catherine has been sheltering Baranov at the Residence. Simon Maryton can't pretend ignorance. He lives there and it wouldn't be plausible. But he's pretty junior. If you, with your rank and experience, had suspected for one moment that she had such an unscheduled guest you'd have been screaming to London on the tie-line. Hugo, whatever you do you mustn't make this look like a put-up job. Do you understand?'

'I understand perfectly, Dick. I'm to be in the audience, and Catherine is to play Joan of Arc. So be it.'

Hugo finished his whisky, put the glass on the side table and walked out of the room. He shut the door very quietly behind him. He was, I knew, in a furious temper.

'Did you have to be so nasty to him, Dick?'

'Yes.' He refilled my glass and sat down opposite me. 'Are you still in love with him? I'd rather hoped – '

'Mind your own damned business!'

He looked at me. 'You're magnificent when you're angry.'

I had to respond. 'Sorry. If you're really interested, the answer is "no". I'm very fond of Hugo – I think I'll always have a – a weakness for him – but, nothing more.'

Dick didn't comment. Instead he said: 'My dear, it's I who should apologize. I'm terribly sorry to have involved you in this mess. If I'd know how badly things were going to turn out I – er – '

'Would have involved me just the same.'

'I'm afraid so. Yes. You were the best possible choice and the issues are too important to make do with second bests. I'll try to explain.'

He paused for almost a full minute, as if to marshal his thoughts. Then he said: 'Last January we heard about certain changes in the Kremlin power structure, and a little later we got hard information about what these changes implied. Although there were no purges or announcements, the hard-liners had effectively taken over. They can't be sure of retaining power indefinitely – even in the Soviet Union checks and balances work eventually – but they're determined, while they've got the chance, to make a last-ditch attempt to take control of Europe. They know NATO's weak and in disarray and they don't think there's a great risk of a real confrontation. In any case, short perhaps of nuclear war they're determined to do everything they can to set up communist-controlled governments in most of the capitals of Europe.'

'But – ' I stammered my incredulity. 'What about the détente? Such a plan's hardly conceivable in present circumstances.'

'That, my dear, is precisely what our closest allies said when we approached them in the greatest secrecy. They refused to believe our source was reliable. They wanted proof. They said they weren't prepared to put the new East-West climate at risk by taking action without proof. We decided, with the utmost reluctance, to bring our agent out of Russia, but before we could do so he died, very conveniently, of a supposed heart attack. He was a White Russian, born in England, and particularly highly-placed in the Soviet hierarchy. And, what's more, he was a very brave man; the last thing he did for us was to arrange to send us the proof we so badly needed. It came in the form of a piece of ultrafiche.' Dick laughed bitterly. 'And thus we were faced with the nice problem of substantiating the ultrafiche, proving the genuineness of the proof. That, Catherine, is where you came in.'

'And Baranov?'

'Yes. Baranov thought he found us, but in fact we found him. He and his Marika were ideal for our purposes. Marika would seem to be a reputable, credible source and the NATO Council could hardly refuse to give the great Baranov a hearing – if he could get so far. We needed a Jeanne d'Arc to get him there. Catherine – '

'I'll do my best, Dick.'

'I know you will, my dear. But, without the ultrafiche – '

Impulsively I held out my hand to him and he took it. I tried to think of something to say that might encourage both of us. 'Perhaps,' I began –

There was a sharp double-knock on the door. 'Not already!' Dick cursed and released my hand. 'I'll have to go. I've got a plane to catch. Iain'll brief you on what has to be done, and he'll tell you about Austria and Operation Overcall.'

'Austria?'

Dick tore a page from a notebook and scribbled hurriedly. 'Give him this, and trust him, Catherine. He'll see you through. When it's all over – '

It was useless to protest that Mr Robinson might not be in a fit state to give me information on anything – or any help in protecting Baranov. Dick was already folding the note and thrusting it into my hand. He bent to kiss me. I must have moved my head because he kissed me squarely on the mouth.

'*Au'voir*, my dear. Take care of yourself.'

'Good luck, Dick.'

Exasperated, I watched the door close behind him. God knows why I had wished him luck. It was I who needed it. I looked at the note I was holding: the temptation to open it and read what he had written was enormous. Pride saved me – and the fact that the paper was folded in an odd way that I might not be able to duplicate. I slipped the note into my bag and drank the last of my champagne.

I wanted to get back to the Residence as soon as possible so as to put my questions to Mr Robinson. Dick's almost casual references were obscure and disturbing. What was Operation Overcall? And how was Austria involved? She wasn't a member of NATO or the Warsaw Pact. Her neutrality had been established in 1955 by the Belvedere Treaty and had never been violated. Irritated by the inconsequence of it all, I had a sudden burst of sympathy with Hugo.

This, however, evaporated very quickly when I returned to the party and discovered that Hugo and Daphne Pewter had gone, leaving me to find my own way home.

Chapter 14

I had no difficulty getting back from the cocktail party at the Embassy. The Brights, as always, rose to the occasion. Po-faced, they accepted my specious excuses for Hugo's departure without me. Lady Bright invited, but didn't press me to share a family meal with them. When I refused, Sir Thomas insisted on sending me home in his own ambassadorial car. They couldn't have been kinder. It was a pity that the ease with which they seemed to overcome all problems only served to lower my morale.

On my return the first thing I did was to deliver the note that Dick had given me. Mr Robinson scrutinized it, opened it and, unless he were a very slow reader, read it at least twice. He then lit a match, set fire to a corner of the paper and, dropping the remains into a convenient glass, stirred them to ashes with a pencil. Such a theatrical gesture was out of character; it bothered me – until I realized that he had done it to impress Baranov, who applauded loudly, clapping his hands.

'Splendid!' he said. 'Everything is splendid. Lady Rayle, Robinson and I have reached a good understanding. I am a quick study and Robinson is a clever coach. Tomorrow I will do the best possible job for him.'

'I wish to God everything was splendid,' Mr Robinson said as he followed me from Simon's rooms to which, as a security measure, Baranov had been moved for the night. 'I telephoned the "safe house" we were staying in, Lady Rayle. Actually, it's a shop with accommodation in the rear and upstairs – very useful. No watch! Nothing was left behind. My men went on Monday night, presumably taking Sergei to you on their way out of Brussels. They didn't say where they were heading, but the – er – shopkeeper's going to make enquiries.'

'It doesn't sound very hopeful.'

'No, especially as I see no reason why they should have the watch.'

'What's the alternative? I suppose a tramp could have found Sergei, but why did he ignore the gold bracelet?'

Mr Robinson disregarded my suggestion. 'Anyway – Dick's orders – we go ahead, ultrafiche or no ultrafiche. We're not done yet.'

We went downstairs to my study. I remembered, with some amusement, the last occasion I had been there with Mr Robinson. It was, in fact, only this afternoon, but it seemed like last month. I offered him a drink, but he refused.

'Dick says I'm to answer all your questions. What do you want to know, Lady Rayle?'

'In the first place, what on earth is Operation Overcall, and what has Austria got to do with it?'

'That's easy enough. Austria's the first Soviet objective. They intend to occupy her early next year, after the elections. Operation Overcall is our response – it's designed to thwart them.'

'But – why Austria, and how?' In spite of what Dick had said I still found it less than credible. 'I know the militant left are agitating, I know about the Opera House, and I know the right are probably over-reacting, but the Russians can't just flout the Belvedere Treaty and walk in. The Treaty guarantees Austria's neutrality.'

'My dear Lady Rayle,' Mr Robinson sighed, pitying my naïveté. 'The scenario will follow the established pattern. The elections will be "proved" to be corrupt and against this background the communists, whatever the real result, will be able to claim a victory for the left. The moderates, naturally, will refuse to yield to power, there'll be riots and fighting in the streets, gutters will allegedly run with blood and the left-wing militants "on the verge of defeat by the fascists" will invite help from the Warsaw Pact. The Soviet Union will be ready and eventually a communist puppet government will be established in Vienna. It's as simple – or as complex – as that!'

It could succeed, I thought. Indeed, what was to stop it? I recalled Czechoslovakia; I even thought of the Reichstag fire. Given a *fait accompli*, everyone would talk but no one would act.

Austria was not even a NATO country, though its neutrality was vital to NATO's defensive position in Central Europe. The Europeans wouldn't risk involvement. The Americans wouldn't send back to Europe the troops they'd just withdrawn. And, given one success, the Russians would try again, until –

As if reading my mind, Mr Robinson said: 'Our only hope is to forestall the Russians. We have to act – we have to be seen to be acting – before it happens, before the take-over – *now*. In other words, Operation Overcall. We've got to bring it off, somehow, Lady Rayle.' He gave me his rare, brilliant smile. 'Tomorrow everything will depend on Baranov – and on you.'

Tomorrow! I would face tomorrow when it came, I told myself, but not before. First we had to get safely through the night. And, shortly after twelve, wearing comfortable, practical clothes, I ensconced myself in an upholstered chair I had moved from one of the bedrooms to an alcove at the top of the main staircase. It was an excellent vantage point.

The sounds of Simon's party floated up to me; some of his friends had left but the rest were still dancing. Upstairs everything was quiet. From time to time I walked around, checking on the rooms and the windows and my two peculiar guests. Baranov, who had announced that he was so excited he would stay awake all night, was softly snoring. Mr Robinson – it had become imperative that he should get some rest – was also sleeping, the sleep of exhaustion. Trying not to think of the fate that could be awaiting Austria, I forced myself to relax.

Suddenly I became conscious that something had changed. The music had stopped. There had been a burst of voices and then silence. I leaned over the balustrade and looked down into the hall. The front door was open; I could even feel the draught. Behind the door Simon and Polly Bright were locked in a close embrace. I went to check on Baranov and Mr Robinson. From one of the windows I watched Polly come out of the house and get into the waiting car – the last car outside the Residence. Simon's party was over.

And Hugo, I realized angrily, had not arrived. We had arranged that he would be here by midnight, but that was before our meeting with Dick Tindle.

I went downstairs. Simon and Rule were clearing glasses and ashtrays from the drawing-room; the houseman and his wife had gone to bed. Rule, who had already had several hours' sleep, was to stay inside the house and patrol the ground floor.

'If you see or hear anything in the least suspicious,' Simon was saying, 'bang on the dinner-gong and someone'll be right with you. Don't mind about waking us up. If it's a false alarm, so much the better.'

Simon, a smear of lipstick at the corner of his mouth, grinned at me. He had obviously enjoyed his party and forgotten about Hugo. I reminded him.

'Damn the man!' he said. 'Lady Rayle, I'm sorry. I should have realized he wasn't here. We'd better telephone. He probably decided to get some sleep and didn't set the alarm.'

But Hugo wasn't asleep. Mr and Mrs Pewter had returned to their residence shortly after eleven. Mrs Pewter had retired at once. Mr Pewter had had his usual late-night whisky and, almost immediately, had gone out again. He had not said when he would return. Mrs Pewter could not be disturbed.

'Well, we'd better take it he's not coming,' I said, in what Guy would have called my don's voice. 'That leaves us rather thin on the ground, doesn't it? Mr Robinson's so exhausted I don't think there's any point in waking him.'

I was more upset than I sounded. I had been counting on Hugo. If the KGB made another attempt to seize Baranov we would be in desperate need of his help – of any help we could get. The next few hours stretched interminably ahead of us and, against my will, black thoughts of tomorrow filled me with pessimism.

I woke up coughing.

The corridor was full of smoke. It was in my eyes and nose and throat. I coughed into my hand, trying not to inhale. In the hall, somebody – Rule, I assumed – was banging on the gong and crying: 'Fire! Fire!' Someone else was hammering on the front door and ringing the bell.

My first thought was for Baranov. With a handkerchief over my mouth and nose I groped my way along the corridor to

Simon's rooms, where both he and Baranov were sleeping. The smoke was thicker here and my eyes were beginning to water badly. I was about to bang on Simon's door when it opened.

'Come on!' said Simon. 'I've just taken Baranov down to the conservatory. We can all go that way. Quick!'

I hesitated. 'No,' I said. 'You go – and look after him.' I wasn't thinking very clearly but I knew my next concern had to be Mr Robinson. The main thing was that the escape route through Simon's rooms was open. Baranov and Simon were both able-bodied, and Simon at least was sensible; they would be all right. Mr Robinson on the other hand was a sick man. But it wouldn't do him any good if I collapsed.

I reached my own door and ran through to my bathroom which was totally free of smoke. I opened the window and took great gulps of cold, damp, wonderful air. Regardless of how much water I spilled I soaked a towel in the handbasin, wrung it out and wrapped it round my head so that there was only a slit for my eyes. As I did this I heard the wail of sirens, first in the distance, then getting louder and louder. Part of my mind registered that Rule must have telephoned the fire brigade before he sounded the gong or shouted his warnings; even so, the response had been very quick.

I hurried from the bathroom, intent on reaching Mr Robinson. On the threshold of the corridor, with the door already open, I paused. I had suddenly remembered that I hadn't shut the bathroom window. The hesitation was fractional; the fire, or whatever it was, wasn't in this part of the house and therefore the draught from the open window was unimportant. But this momentary pause meant that through the thinning smoke I saw two dark forms with gas-masks and firemen's helmets reach the top of the stairs.

They didn't see me. They were too busy doing something with their hands. There were a couple of almost simultaneous flares, like flames from a big cigar lighter, and, as the men turned away from me, one of them seemed to drop something in the alcove where minutes ago I had been asleep.

And more, new smoke began to pour into the corridor.

I didn't stop to investigate. I ran. Luckily Mr Robinson had been given a room in one of the side passages, well away from the suite which, I was sure, the 'firemen' would be making for – the suite which Baranov had occupied before tonight. Not bothering to knock, I burst into the room.

'Wake up!' I said. 'Hurry! Hurry!'

My voice was muffled by the towel round my head and in the dim light from the passage I must have looked a strange sight. What happened next was totally unexpected. One moment I was shaking Mr Robinson by the shoulders and the next I was flat on my back across the bed with something sharp pricking the skin beneath my chin.

At least I had the sense not to struggle. And, realizing somewhat belatedly who I was, he let me go. 'Don't ever wake me like that again, Lady Rayle,' he said, in a dead flat voice. Then calmly he began to clean his nails with the file he had been holding at my throat.

'Another time I'll gladly let you burn,' I said. 'Now I may need you. The house is full of smoke. There may or may not be a fire. The brigade has arrived, but a couple of the firemen seem to be Russians, looking for Baranov. So put on some clothes, Mr Robinson, and let's get out of here.'

To give him his due, he didn't quibble. He was dressed by the time I had the towels ready and, for all his bravado, was sitting on the bed. He wasn't feeling as well as he pretended. He swayed a little when he stood up and I hoped he wasn't going to faint.

'Where's Baranov?'

'I don't know. But Simon's with him. So come on and don't try any heroics.'

We had reached the top of the stairs when from the far end of the corridor there was a loud report, followed instantaneously by a sharp, cracking sound. It was the second time I had heard such a noise in the last few minutes and, though I couldn't place it, I instinctively associated it with the Russians. It was not a reassuring noise.

A fireman, gesturing to us to get out of the house, went off to investigate, and we hurried down to the hall. Another fireman passed us on the stairs and a third disappeared into the servants' quarters. I thought they were all genuine, but there was no way of being sure.

The front door was wide open and the smoke was dissipating. Mr Robinson pulled the towel off his head. He held me back.

'When we get outside I'm going to disappear. If I can find Baranov and Simon I'll stay with them until the excitement's over, so don't expect to see me for a while.'

He was gone before I could object. He would probably collapse somewhere, and who was to form the search party? Except for a lot of strangers, and God knew which of those I could trust, I was alone. I followed him out of the front door.

Immediately I was floodlit, or that was how it seemed. In the headlights of an assembly of vehicles everything here was as bright as in a football stadium – and as busy. There were fire engines, an ambulance, several cars and a motley gathering of people, most of them in various uniforms. They were either standing in clusters, talking, or running about. Everyone was occupied, though nobody appeared to be doing anything about the fire.

And there was a fire! I could smell burning and see smoke, dirty, black smoke, coming from the corner of the house. That was where the fire-hoses snaking across the flower-bed were leading, towards my study, where there was yet more activity. I started in that direction and someone called my name.

The houseman was more voluble than usual. He and his wife had been woken by the noise of the fire engines. His wife was in the ambulance with the Rules. It was cold and they had taken shelter there. Everybody was all right. Rule was quite recovered but he had been worried about me and Mr Maryton.

Rule himself was more explicit. 'I'd just done my rounds, my lady, and I was making a cup of tea when I thought I heard some glass breaking. Then I smelt the smoke. It was everywhere, sudden-like. I banged on the gong and I was coming up for you but there was somebody at the front door. I managed to open it before the smoke got to me, and when I came to I was lying out on the drive.'

I refrained from telling him that nothing had 'got to' him

until he had opened the door. Considering that I had been asleep, I couldn't reproach him for not having been more on his guard; his reactions had been natural. Besides, he would only have delayed, not prevented, the Russians from gaining free access to the Residence.

As I climbed out of the ambulance a fireman asked me if I were the Ambassador. He said his Commandant would be grateful for a word with me, which was precisely what I wanted too. It was impossible to make any plans before I knew what damage had been done and what, if any, privacy we could expect for the rest of the night. This was a priority.

But I was twice delayed on my way to the Commandant. The butler of my German neighbour, who was something to do with the Common Market, suddenly appeared to offer his master's sympathy and hospitality. Then what I first mistook for a child darted out from behind a police car, and stood squarely in front of me.

'Catherine!'

'Daphne – what on earth?'

'Where's Hugo?'

'I haven't the least idea.'

'Don't lie to me! He promised he wouldn't go to you tonight, but he meant to all the time. He put something in my drink, but I woke up just the same – and he was gone.' She was spitting with anger.

'Hugo's not here, Daphne. I haven't seen him since the Brights' party. You'd better go home.'

'So that when the fire's out you can go back to bed – you and Hugo?'

I was angry then. I would have pushed past her, left her to her suspicions, but she held on to my arm. She was so much smaller that I could still have knocked her aside if I had been prepared to use force. But that would have meant a scene. She would probably have screamed at me. With an effort I controlled my own temper.

'Daphne, I give you my word – '

'Your word! You do take me for a fool, don't you, Catherine?

Do you really believe I've swallowed all that rubbish about some Russian dancer defecting to *you*? And the KGB trying to get him back? I admit the tights convinced me for a while but you could have bought them anywhere. That's what the chap at the Russian Embassy said.'

'You bitch!' I was trembling. 'You utter bitch!'

So much had now become clear, appallingly clear. Although he had denied it, Hugo had told Daphne about Baranov. He had told her the truth and she hadn't believed him. He had even taken Albrecht's tights from Simon's room in order to convince her, but without success. She was mad with jealousy, so mad that she had been prepared to tell the Russians that Baranov was at the Residence. If it hadn't been for her they might never have known.

'It's you that's the bitch,' Daphne said savagely. 'I hate you, Catherine. I hate you. I always have, long before you came to Brussels. Hugo's slept with other women, I know, but you're the only one he's ever lived with, the one he meant to marry. He swore it was somebody else but I knew it was you, and I made him admit it. Now you're trying to get him back. You won't succeed. I'm his wife. He'll never leave me.'

'Go home, Daphne.' My voice shook but I spoke gently. My anger had evaporated as quickly as it had flared. Her words had been too revealing. I felt pity for her, and a certain amount of revulsion. 'Go home!' I repeated.

'I'm going,' she said, 'but I'm taking Hugo with me.'

She cursed me and ran. The last I saw of her she was jumping over the hosepipes that lay across the flower-bed. She was going towards the front door, presumably to look for Hugo.

'*Excellence*.'

I turned to the fireman who was waiting to escort me to his Commandant. He had been standing a few feet from Daphne and me, but we had kept our voices low – we had been practically hissing at each other – and we had been speaking English. It was improbable that he had understood what we had been saying. Which meant that there was no witness to Daphne's admission of treachery. But did that matter? Was I going to accuse

Daphne? I had no idea. Later, I thought, later I'll decide what to do about her. It can wait. She's done all the damage she can for the moment.

My immediate concern was with the Commandant and, it seemed, a Commissaire de police. They were charming, considerate but rather troubled men. They assured me that the fire was confined to one room – my study, that it was under control and almost out, that little harm had been done to the Residence, that as soon as the smoke had cleared we could return inside. I thanked them and waited. They looked at each other. Neither wanted to be the one to break the bad news to me.

The Commandant lost. '*Excellence*, I regret, but you must prepare yourself for a shock – a very grave shock. We are dealing here with a case of arson. We have proof that fire bombs, small incendiaries, were tossed through the window into your study. There is also evidence that smoke canisters, possibly fired from a riot gun like gas grenades, were shot through some of the upstairs windows and we have found the remains of smoke candles inside the house. The last implies intruders.'

I did my best to appear shocked. In fact, apart from the technical details, I had learnt nothing I had not already suspected. But I was daunted by the Russians' efficiency and determination. I shivered.

'You're cold, *Excellence*. We'll arrange for a wrap to be fetched.'

'That's very kind of you.' I smiled my appreciation, thankful that the casual clothes I was wearing were such as I might have flung on when roused from sleep by an alarm of fire. A coat over a nightdress might have looked more natural, but at least my appearance didn't arouse curiosity.

'There is also the point, *Excellence*, that the locks of two of the first floor rooms seem to have been blown off,' he said. 'I haven't yet ascertained how.'

'Good heavens!' This was news, though I remembered the loud, cracking noise that Mr Robinson and I had heard as we reached the stairs. 'Gentlemen, I'm appalled. I – I don't know what to say.'

'You have no idea, *Excellence*, what the intruders might have been seeking? Obviously it is something of importance for them to have taken these extreme measures. They were by no means common thieves.'

I shook my head. 'I have some papers here, of course, but they're mostly personal. They have no intrinsic value. And they're certainly not secret or vital to NATO in any way. I wouldn't have thought that anyone would want to steal them, though it's true we did have some would-be burglars a few days ago.'

And I was telling him about the pseudo-maintenance men – the houseman and his wife would be sure to mention them – when a fireman arrived to report that the fire was completely extinguished. The Commandant excused himself just as the houseman appeared with my fur coat. There was a certain amount of confusion. The firemen began to roll up their hoses. The Commissaire went to use his radio-telephone. I huddled into the comfort of my mink.

'Kit! Oh, thank God!'

Without any warning I found myself in a close embrace. I gasped as Hugo clutched me desperately, half lifting me off my feet. His breath, heavy with whisky, was unpleasant. I struggled to free myself.

'Are you drunk?' I said angrily.

'Thank God you're all right. I was passing the gates when a fire engine drove out. I was scared as hell.'

'Passing the gates? You were meant to be here, to help, Hugo. And where have you been, anyway? Daphne's been looking for you.'

'Daphne?'

'Yes. Daphne – your wife. I told her to go home. You'd better go too.'

'Kit, I'm sorry about tonight. But first there was that bloody man Tindle. Then I had a row with Daphne – about you. So I went downtown, around the bars. I – '

'It doesn't matter now, Hugo.'

'But Kit – for God's sake! Tell me what's happened. Where's Simon and – '

We were interrupted by Mr Robinson, looking as if only will-power kept him on his feet.

'You didn't find them?'

'No,' Mr Robinson said flatly. 'I tried everywhere. No sign of either of them. But I did find someone.' Surprisingly, he took hold of my arm. 'Lady Rayle, there's a woman I've never seen before lying at the bottom of Simon's staircase. Her neck's broken.'

Chapter 15

'She's dead. You can't do anything for her.'

Mr Robinson gripped Hugo by the elbow and Hugo winced with pain, but he didn't try to pull his arm free. He stood, breathing heavily. He had known at once that the crumpled body at the bottom of Simon's winding stairs was Daphne. There had been no doubt in my mind, either. We hadn't needed Mr Robinson's one-line description – a *petite* blonde, thirty-five or so, married, expensive.

'Listen,' Mr Robinson said. 'The police will find her very soon. When they do, they'll ask a lot of questions and we've got to have the right answers. So concentrate! We haven't much time.'

We had, in fact, something under five minutes. Mr Robinson didn't waste a second of them. He spoke very fast and without repeating himself, except when he wanted to ensure that we had fully grasped what he had been saying. The interruption still came too soon.

'*Excellence!*'

Our time was up. Mr Robinson's hand slid from Hugo's elbow to his shoulder, and he leaned on him as if in need of support. It was my cue. I couldn't see Hugo's face because it was in shadow and, apart from once jerking out Daphne's name, he hadn't uttered a word. I prayed that he would be able to control himself.

'Ah, you're the man I want,' I said to the Commissaire de police. 'I wonder if I could ask you a favour. Mr Robinson was going back to the Hôtel Dieu later in the day, but all this excitement has upset him. He's feeling very unwell. Could you possibly get the ambulance to take him to the hospital now?'

There was an appreciable pause before he answered. 'But of course, *Excellence*. Mr Robinson must go at once. I will call another immediately.'

'Another? Another ambulance?'

'Yes, *Excellence*. We may require one for an accident case.'

'An accident? Has one of the firemen been hurt?'

'No, *Excellence*. A woman has fallen down some back stairs.' He referred to a notebook, shining a torch on it. 'Short, fair-haired, blue-eyed, between thirty and forty years – '

'Oh God! Kit, that sounds like Daphne. You said she was here.' To my relief Hugo was showing precisely the right amount of anxiety and agitation. He turned to the Commissaire. 'It could be Daphne – my wife. Where is she? Is she badly hurt?'

'I'm sorry, Lady Rayle, sorry. Going to faint.'

Mr Robinson had spoken in English but the Commissaire, I noticed, was quicker than Hugo to help him and lower him to the gravel of the driveway.

The Commissaire then raised an arm and two of his men appeared as if by magic. A stretcher was produced and Mr Robinson was borne away; I had no idea if his faint was genuine. I turned to the Commissaire. 'This is beyond belief,' I said.

'*Excellence*, please. If you will allow me, things will arrange themselves.'

And, indeed, in the course of the next half-hour things did arrange themselves, at least as well as we had any right to expect. Hugo was led gently away to identify Daphne's body and make a formal statement. The firemen departed, leaving my study something of a shambles, but that was a minimal concern. The police searched the Residence and pronounced it free of intruders; they insisted on establishing a patrol in the grounds, which I'd have welcomed if it hadn't been for the unknown whereabouts of Simon and Baranov. And, mindful of Mr Robinson's advice not to lie unless it were essential, I answered the Commissaire's inevitable questions with what I hoped was a nice blend of helpfulness in unusual circumstances and expectation of diplomatic privilege.

In the event the Commissaire was co-operative. I had no trouble and he had almost finished his questioning when, to my surprise, the houseman announced a telephone call for me from Miss Polly Bright.

'Polly – my dear! Is something wrong?'

'Lady Rayle, I'm most terribly sorry to bother you like this.' Her voice sounded theatrically unreal. 'Simon told me to get hold of Rule. But when your houseman said you'd had a fire at the Residence I thought perhaps I should speak to you – in case you had some message for Simon.'

'Yes, how very sensible of you,' I said, trying to think quickly. 'We were lucky the fire wasn't serious. It's out now and the firemen have gone. But the police are still here.' I smiled apologetically at the Commissaire, who was pretending not to listen to my conversation. 'They'll probably be here some time. There's been a dreadful accident, Polly. Daphne – Mrs Pewter – fell downstairs and I'm afraid she's dead.'

'Oh God! I – I'm terribly sorry.'

In my anxiety to give Simon as much information as possible I had forgotten that Daphne's death would be a shock to Polly. 'But, my dear, what about you?' I said hurriedly. 'You haven't told me why you want Rule at this time of the morning.'

'It's so stupid of us, Lady Rayle. But after the party we decided to go for a drive and we were coming back along the Chaussée de la Hulpe when we ran out of petrol. We're stranded.' Polly paused. 'And, what with the fire and poor Mrs Pewter, I suppose you need Simon.'

'Oh no, there's nothing he can do here for the moment,' I said casually. 'Nevertheless, we must rescue you. If you tell me exactly where you are I'll send Rule with some petrol. Then perhaps Simon can bring you back here for an early breakfast.'

Polly thanked me profusely, but she wasn't sure about breakfast. I understood. They would wait for Rule and, from what he could add to the information I had given Polly, Simon would make his decision. But where else could they take Baranov, if Simon decided not to return to the Residence? Baranov couldn't come to NATO unwashed, unshaved and in his pyjamas. And what was Polly doing with them? God knows what Tommy Bright would say, if he ever heard about it.

I turned to the Commissaire and apologized for the interruption. I explained that my Private Secretary and his fiancée, daughter of Her Majesty's Ambassador to Belgium, were stranded in their car on the Chaussée de la Hulpe not far from where it joined the Route de Mont-Saint-Jean. I asked his permission to send my chauffeur with petrol.

'Immediately, *Excellence*. It's always good to be young and in love, but at this time of year it's cold in the Forêt during the night.'

In spite of the central heating, which was warming the house again, and the fact that I was still wearing my mink coat, I felt the chill on my back. With an effort I suppressed a shiver. The place Polly had described, the place where she was waiting with Simon and – presumably – Baranov, was in the Forêt de Soignes. It couldn't be very far from where Sergei's body lay rotting in its ditch.

Rule, returning to the Residence alone, reported that Simon, now his car was going, would take Polly home; he would telephone later but, unless I wanted him, would go straight to the office.

It was a fairly cryptic message – I couldn't really believe that Simon had taken Baranov to the Brights – but there was nothing I could do about it, nothing I could do about anything for the moment; and I was exhausted. I went up to my room. Though I wouldn't have thought it possible, I was asleep almost at once.

The telephone's persistent ringing forced me to return to wakefulness, but I had slept for the greater part of two hours. As consciousness flooded back the sound of Simon's voice on the line was encouraging; things weren't as bad as they might have been. At least we had kept Baranov safe, and if only all went well today . . .

'Lady Rayle? It's Simon. I'm sorry to disturb you, but I wondered if you needed me?'

'No, not particularly. Is everything all right with you?'

'Thank you, yes. Everything's fine. But there must be a pile of work waiting for me at the office and I don't imagine Hugo will be in today. I thought I'd go along and get an early start as soon as Polly has made me some breakfast.'

'Yes, that's a good idea.'

'There's only one problem, Lady Rayle. I wonder if you'd do

me a favour. I'm still in the gear I wore for that party last night. Could you possibly bring me a clean shirt and maybe something more suitable for NATO? I know it's awful cheek to ask you, but if you wouldn't mind – '

'Very well, though I'm not sure how soon I'll be in. You'd better cancel all my appointments, except the one with the Secretary General. And there are a couple of phone calls I'd like you to make – both concerned with Mr Robinson. He collapsed during the night – the excitement of the fire and Daphne's death – and an ambulance took him back to the Hôtel Dieu. Phone the matron, will you, Simon, and give her my apologies? Explain to her – I've already explained it to the police – that if I'd not taken him flowers he wouldn't have known my name; he was confused between the British Ambassador and the NATO Permrep and he didn't realize I wasn't the right person for him to come to. Say that his memory seems to be improving and he's sure he's a British national. Our consul will be able to help him.' I paused. Mr Robinson had told me to contact Dick's people; they were to get him out of the hospital and out of the country, quickly but by legitimate means. 'Then, phone the consulate and tell them what's happened.'

I put down the receiver. Simon's request for clothes was something of a problem. I took it he meant for Baranov as well as for himself, and if so I must do what I could to find something suitable. As soon as I had bathed and dressed I went along to Simon's rooms.

The shattered door was a reminder of the Russians' violence. If it hadn't been for Daphne – but Daphne had paid for her jealousy, too dearly. She had died in horrible, unhappy circumstances, and the fact that it was she who had pointed the KGB at the Residence wasn't relevant any more. Her treachery was best forgotten.

I passed through Simon's sitting-room, which looked perfectly normal; there was no sign of any disturbance. But on the threshold of the bedroom I stopped short. The place was chaotic. Suits had been thrown from the cupboards to lie where they had fallen. Shelves had been emptied on to the floor. Drawers had been opened and their contents tossed aside. It had been a hurried and thorough search.

'What on earth – ' I said aloud, though I guessed the answer. The KGB men had clearly searched for proof of Baranov's presence. I thrust from my mind the thought that Daphne might have interrupted them, and sorted through the clothing. I found a dark suit and tie for Simon, but there seemed nothing to fit Baranov. What was more, I realized suddenly, the KGB had found its proof; Albrecht's costume had disappeared. I quickly pushed a random selection of garments into a case, and took it to my room.

Over breakfast I thought about the day ahead.

And later, as Rule drove me to the office, I made a mental list of things to be done.

It was inevitable that Daphne's death and the arson would give rise to a certain amount of publicity; the Press Secretary would be the man to deal with that. A telegram must go to the FCO about Baranov, and another about the attack on the Residence; probably Simon was already drafting these. He could also arrange for the repair work. Someone – it would have to be David Driscole – must stand in for Hugo.

And Hugo himself? He had gone home, making it clear that he needed no help. But he couldn't be left alone with his grief and self-searching – and all the practical problems of Daphne's death. I thought of Simon again, but they weren't nearly as close as they had been; besides, Simon was young and inappropriately happy with his Polly. Which reminded me of the Brights. Lady Bright hadn't liked Daphne, but both she and Tommy got on well with Hugo . . .

Rule was passing the guardpost at the entrance to NATO Headquarters, and the guards were saluting smartly as I put a mental line under my list. With one exception – letting Dick know what was happening – they were things to be done by others. I had reserved for myself what was really important – Baranov, the Secretary General, the Council.

First, however, I was to have one pleasant surprise. Simon and Baranov were waiting for me in my office. Simon, his face and hands badly scratched, was wearing jeans and a sweater; he looked disreputable. Baranov, on the contrary, was dressed in a beautifully-cut suit, a silk shirt and patent leather shoes. He was preening himself like a peacock.

'Do I not look splendid, Lady Rayle?' he said.

'Yes, indeed.' I nodded my approval.

'We've come from Lena's, Lady Rayle,' Simon said. 'You know, the singer from Le Domaine who borrowed that Mercedes for us the night we picked up Baranov. If I'd had any sense we'd have gone there at once, instead of driving half way to Paris. Her boy-friend's exactly the same size as Baranov and everything fitted. You can see I wasn't so lucky.'

I arranged for my secretary to look after Baranov for a while and told Simon to start again from the beginning.

'After I left you, I followed Baranov down to the conservatory,' he said, 'and we went out into the garden. I wasn't sure what to do. I guessed the Russians had started the fire and I knew we had to hide. The question was where. I was making for the maze when we nearly ran into a couple of the comrades who appeared from nowhere. So I forced a way through the hedge – hence all these scratches – and we went up the hill through the Germans' garden, which seemed a lot safer than ours. And Polly was waiting in her car.'

'By chance?'

'Not exactly.' Simon laughed. 'It had occurred to me that if something did happen in the night we might need an escape route, and I asked Polly to leave her car at the end of the lane. I hoped no one would recognize it.'

'That was clever of you. But what did you tell her?'

'I told her we had a – a VIP staying at the Residence and he might want to leave privately. I expected to find the car. I didn't expect to find Polly in it. But – ' Simon made a helpless gesture. 'Anyway, you can trust Polly.'

'And Lena?'

'Lena was fabulous! She provided baths, electric razor, breakfast, and a complete outfit for Baranov.' He stopped. 'You can trust Lena too, Lady Rayle. Hugo's been a good friend to her and her brother. She'd do anything for him.'

'Yes. I realize that.' I swallowed a mixture of emotions; unknowingly Simon had just prompted an idea. 'What about

Daphne? How – how did she and Lena get on?'

'Daphne?' Simon was taken aback, as well he might have been. 'I don't – they didn't have much to do with each other. Why do you ask, Lady Rayle?'

'Because . . .'

I had already made up my mind that nobody – and nobody, for very different reasons, included both Hugo Pewter and Dick Tindle – should ever suspect Daphne's treachery or what had motivated it. But I knew that I had to satisfy Simon, who would worry at a loose end.

'Simon, it – it was Hugo who took Albrecht's tights from your room. He borrowed them to prove to Daphne that he hadn't been spending all his time the last few days with Lena.'

'What? Oh – Christ! It – it wasn't like that at all.'

'He must never suspect you know,' I said hurriedly.

'No. No, of course not. Poor old Hugo!'

And poor, pathetic Daphne, I thought.

But I knew what Dick Tindle would say: Hugo and Daphne didn't really matter. None of us mattered. Only Operation Overcall. That was important. That did matter.

Chapter 16

Mr Robinson had said: 'Everything will depend on Baranov and you,' but what with the strain of the past few days – culminating last night in the fire and Daphne's death – it was only now, when I was on the point of taking Baranov to the Secretary General, that the full import of these words hit me. I was chilled. I was also determined. If Operation Overcall failed, it wouldn't be because of me or, if I could help it, because of Baranov.

At ten minutes to eleven, having made sure that Baranov had his *laissez-passer* – the green form which entitled him to be inside NATO headquarters if escorted by someone with a permanent NATO pass – we left the Delegation for the office of the Secretary General. My appointment was for the hour and we didn't have to wait.

As we came in the Secretary General rose from behind his desk, frowning and hesitant when he saw I was not alone. I had expected this; I had no right to bring a stranger into his office without warning, and Baranov, after all, was a Soviet defector. Hugo, however, had suggested that my best chance was to take the Secretary General by surprise and I had deliberately committed the breach of protocol. I hurried to introduce the two men.

'Mr Secretary General, may I present Monsieur Baranov, formerly of the Bolshoi Ballet Company.'

This was a delicate moment. The Secretary General, shocked at the identity of his unexpected visitor, could refuse to meet Baranov and ask us to leave immediately; I had put him in an abominable position. Or Baranov, even though I had warned him that Marika's future depended on 'a good performance', could take offence at a chilly welcome and begin to sulk. Yet it was essential that they shouldn't antagonize each other from the outset. My mouth was dry with apprehension.

I need not have worried. The Secretary General coped magnificently. His face lit up with pleasure. He came from behind his desk, his arm outstretched. It was a genuine gesture of admiration, to which Baranov responded gracefully. They shook hands and the Secretary General led us to a cluster of armchairs where we could talk in comfort.

'This is an occasion for me,' he said. 'I have long admired the wonderful dancing of Monsieur Baranov. Perhaps – it is very early, I know, but can I offer you a drink?'

'Thank you,' Baranov said. 'Champagne.'

The Secretary General, who was an abstemious man and considered a small glass of sherry before lunch an indulgence, didn't blanch. 'Certainly,' he said. 'I will order it at once. Will you excuse me?'

He didn't use the intercom, but went through into his secretary's office. He was gone several minutes. It was a relief when he returned.

'It will not be long,' he said. He looked at me blandly. 'I have taken the liberty of asking the Assistant Secretary General for Plans and Policy to join us. You do not mind, Catherine?'

'Not at all,' I said. 'As you surmised, Johan, this isn't really a social visit. Monsieur Baranov has something of the utmost importance to tell you, something I'm convinced the whole Council should hear.'

Still smiling, he nodded at me. He didn't query my statement. He went across to his desk, fiddled in a drawer, and came back to sit with us. I suspected that he had turned on a tape-recorder. He was a careful man, nobody's fool.

He said conversationally to Baranov: 'I had the great pleasure of watching you dance Albrecht last Friday evening when, alas, you were taken ill. I hope you are quite recovered.'

'I was not ill,' Baranov said. 'But my chance came and I seized it. You understand, when the Bolshoi dances in the West I am always watched very closely. I fled. I ran through the back streets behind the Théâtre Royal de la Monnaie until I saw a taxi. I bribed him to take me to the British Residence, to Lady Rayle.'

'You are asking the British for asylum?'

'Asylum! What is this asylum?'

Baranov was on his feet, looking down on us. He poured forth a stream of Russian. The Secretary General glanced at me questioningly and I shook my head. I remembered that the Assistant Secretary General spoke Russian fluently, and he had come into the room. He was standing now, with his back against the closed door. He was carrying a tray with four glasses and an ice bucket containing a bottle of champagne. It was a surreal situation.

For some reason Baranov switched to English. 'I ask for nothing,' he said. 'I am Baranov. I go to Israel to be with my love, my Marika, whom I am to marry. But first I risk my life, Baranov's life, to come to *you*, Mr Secretary General, because Marika says Austria must be saved. Austria is a small country like Israel, and NATO must not allow the Soviet Union to gobble up Austria!' As suddenly as he had stood, he sat. 'Good.' He smiled. 'I like champagne.'

He could have been absurd, but he wasn't. He was very impressive. Even I, who by this time was accustomed to Baranov's dramatics and had known more or less what he would say, was impressed. The two men were astounded. That a world-famous ballet dancer should want to defect was one thing, but that he should explode a political bombshell in their midst was something else again. Whatever credence they might ultimately give to his story, at least they were now determined to hear it.

We had made a splendid start.

That our luck didn't hold wasn't Baranov's fault. He told his story simply but vividly; he had been right when he said that he was a quick study and Mr Robinson a clever coach. It didn't take very long. He only gave them the bare bones and they let him finish without interruption. Then the questions began, gentle enough but probing. And Baranov had the answers.

'Monsieur Baranov, this information about the Russians' plan to take over Austria – you have it on the authority of your fiancée, Marika. Am I right?'

'Yes. And what more would you ask? Marika, though she is Jewish, is – was – the personal assistant – you could say the confidante – of the official who co-ordinates arms production for the Soviet Union and its satellites.'

'Yet she was prepared to - I hesitated to use the word - betray her country like this?'

'It is no betrayal! She knows it to be wicked madness for Russia to attack Austria in this way. She believes that if the Russians are not stopped now they will soon try to attack some other country, just as Hitler did in the 'thirties. And then inevitably there will be war – a big war.'

'Where is Marika at present?'

'On her way to Israel. Perhaps already in Tel Aviv. We arranged to meet at the home of some Jewish friends who were allowed to leave Moscow a few months ago. And my one desire is to be with her. I myself am not a political being. I am Baranov. But she besought me to come to NATO.'

'And she gave you proof of what you were to tell us, Monsieur Baranov? She gave you this ultrafiche hidden in a watch? You have it with you?'

'Niet!'

I had almost seen their hands outstretched, waiting to take possession of the factual evidence. But at the flat Russian negative, the gestures became tokens of resignation. They exchanged glances. Then, without apology, they spoke rapidly, each in his own language but with complete understanding of the other, as Scandinavians do.

'May we enquire what has happened to the microfilm?' the Secretary General asked finally. 'Have we a hope of seeing it, or is it lost?'

There was no trace of sarcasm in his words but I knew at once that he had suspended belief. Baranov, however, took the questions literally. He explained. Because he feared that he himself was suspected by the KGB he had given the watch to Sergei Alexandrov, his friend, who had hoped to come with him to Israel.

'And now I do not know where the watch is, or Sergei,' Baranov said. 'On the first night, after *Swan Lake*, we did not leave the theatre together. When I got back to the Embassy I was tired and I went straight to bed. I'd only been asleep for a few minutes when I was made to get up and I was questioned. We were all questioned. The KGB men said the car had stopped at some lights and Sergei had jumped out and run away, but I am sure it was not like that. He would never go off without warning me and returning the watch. I believe they had seized him and were holding him themselves.'

There were some more questions but they had lost their edge. Obviously the Secretary General now wanted to confer with his advisers and those Permreps he trusted most. They in turn would want to talk to Baranov and to their capitals. I decided to make a tactical withdrawal. If nothing else it would demonstrate that I had no objection to leaving Baranov to face an interrogation by himself.

'Johan, you understand my position,' I said. 'You know what I want – an emergency Council meeting as soon as possible, and I'll propose that Monsieur Baranov should be heard. It's up to you.'

'Yes, yes, Catherine. I understand. You request an emergency meeting,' he said, and I could see him groping for the right words. 'But this is not – not an official British Government request, no?'

'No – not yet.' Suspecting the depth of the diplomatic waters, he was content to leave it at that for the moment, and I continued. 'In the meantime there are arrangements to be made. At the very least, after he has risked so much, I'm determined that Monsieur Baranov shall get to Israel. I must see the Israelis and the Belgians, and consult with London. May I leave him with you? I'll send Mr Maryton to bring him back to the Delegation as soon as you've finished.'

They agreed with some signs of relief, and I hurried through the long, anonymous NATO corridors to my office. Simon, who had been gnawing his nails with anxiety and curiosity, was waiting for me. When I told him what had happened, he seemed to think things had gone well, but I was depressed and he tried to cheer me.

'They can't completely disregard what Baranov has to say, Lady Rayle. They can't believe he's invented the whole thing. Why on earth should he? After all, he is Baranov. And there's quite a lot of supporting evidence.'

But I had seen those two faces grow blank when Baranov explained that he didn't have the ultrafiche, and I knew that without it his story was worth no more than Marika's word, and by itself that would warrant no action. There would be a lot of talk and conferring and consultation but nothing would be done about Austria – until it was too late. I felt desperate.

I had finished my lunch – sandwiches I didn't want and a cup of coffee – when I was officially informed that later in the afternoon an emergency meeting of the Council would be held at my request. It would be an executive session, in private and without an agenda. Then the Assistant Secretary General telephoned to suggest that I should have my friend 'in readiness'. He said no more, but it was a crumb of comfort. Evidently Baranov's information was not to be dismissed out of hand.

By the time I entered the Council chamber, however, I had a sense of doom and, as I took my place in alphabetical order at the round, centreless table, between the places reserved for the Turkish and United States Permreps, I received little encouragement. My colleagues either acknowledged me too politely or managed to avoid catching my eye. Only the Belgian Permrep, who had been very helpful in contacting the Israeli Ambassador and trying to regularize Baranov's position in Brussels, gave me a warm smile.

If Hugo had been sitting behind me I would have been much happier. Indeed, anybody from the UK Delegation would have given me moral support. But, since this was a closed session of the Council, the Permanent Representatives or their Deputies sat alone, without the usual complement of advisers, and I could feel the draught on my back.

I was glad when the United States Permrep took his seat beside me. The American was a heavy, slow-moving man. There was, however, nothing heavy or slow-moving about his mind; he was very able indeed. I liked and respected him; he liked me, period. He thought that in my present job I was a joke, and potentially a dangerous one – or so I guessed. Nevertheless, he had always been helpful and kind and I had rather hoped that he would have approached me before this meeting – the Americans inevitably have enormous influence on the decisions of the Council, and his support could make all the difference. But he hadn't, and I had decided against making the first advance.

Now he said: 'Catherine! I've just been talking to your protégé and I'm overwhelmed. My, but he was lucky he defected to you and not to one of the other Permreps, wasn't he? I could name one or two who wouldn't have given him a hearing over this Austrian business.'

I shrugged. 'In that case, Seymour, we were all lucky, weren't we? In fact, Baranov came to me because he knew I'd at least be sympathetic to him. I met him at the reception the Belgian Government gave for the Bolshoi, and someone told him I was a friend of Anna de Lisle's.'

'Ah, yes!'

He nodded, as if his question and its implications had been trivial, but I realized that the point had bothered him. I wondered how many more seemingly unimportant questions I would be asked before the day was out – and if there were any among them for which I would have no answer. Luckily I had little time to worry.

The Secretary General, part of whose job is to act as Chairman of the Council, was calling the meeting to order. He said I had asked for an emergency meeting to discuss the position of the Federal Republic of Austria, a neutral country but nevertheless a country whose geographic position made her territory vital to the defence of the West. He called on me to explain the situation.

Normally this would have been simple. These meetings are very informal, quite unlike the United Nations. Speakers remain seated in their places and do not orate from a rostrum. People call each other by their first names, and questions and interruptions are routine. There is rarely any overt hostility, and then usually over financial rather than strategic matters. For me, however, today was different; so much depended on the result. The whole thing had become an ordeal.

Once again I began my story, or rather Baranov's story. I told it as straightforwardly as possible. I made no attempt to shock – if anything I underplayed it – but everyone listened with the closest attention. I was mindful of the American's earlier query, and I covered every point that I – or Mr Robinson – had been able to think of, but of course there were questions.

'I don't quite understand how the KGB knew that Baranov was at your Residence,' the Italian Ambassador said.

'One can only assume that when he fled from the theatre he was followed.'

'Do you think they made these extraordinary attacks on you – especially the dreadful fire last night – to recapture Baranov because he is a great, international figure or because they had reason to believe he was bringing secret information to the West?' asked the Danish Permrep.

'I have no idea. But does it matter? Isn't the important thing that we should all hear what Baranov himself has to say about Austria?'

'It's most unusual for the Council to be seized of an allegedly emergency situation in this way,' said the Canadian Permrep. 'I hope Lady Rayle won't object if I suggest that we all realize she might take an unorthodox approach to the arrival of a famous Soviet defector on her doorstep – and one apparently bearing gifts of this nature for NATO. But we've heard nothing of all this through normal channels, and I'm afraid I really must ask the extent to which the British Ambassador is presenting an official British position.' He sat back, with a benign smile.

I knew what the Canadian was thinking. He had known Hugo well in various capitals over the years, and he couldn't believe that I was acting with the backing of the Delegation or the Foreign and Commonwealth Office. It was an issue I had hoped to avoid, but I saw my opportunity. Speaking as though my mouth were full of dry ice, I said:

'Her Majesty's Government have the matter under advisement. They were not informed until this morning, immediately before I met with the Secretary General. For the record, my Deputy, Mr Pewter, knew nothing about Baranov until last night when he and his wife arrived at the fire in which she subsequently died. The only member of my Delegation who had any knowledge of the affair was Simon Maryton, my Private Secretary, who lives in the Residence. What I did, I did on my own authority. I believe it was the right thing to do. This intelligence was offered to NATO and it is something for NATO as a whole to deal with, not for one member to wrap up in diplomatic tape.

I only pray that NATO will have the courage to take action before it's too late and the Soviet Union has engulfed Austria and established an impregnable position in central Europe.'

My nerves stretched, I sat in my place, listening to the silence in the Council chamber. Then someone cleared his throat. At once there was a murmur of conversation. I yearned for a drink, but my hand was trembling so much that I didn't dare lift the water glass in front of me. The Secretary General called the meeting to order and the American Ambassador – silently I blessed him – proposed that Baranov should be asked to address us. While we waited for Baranov to be brought in, the ambassadors talked among themselves.

Leaning towards me Seymour said: 'That was a good speech, Catherine, a good speech. You're a brave woman.'

It wasn't easy to smile at him. I had done my best, as I had promised Dick Tindle, but I was not Jeanne d'Arc and without the ultrafiche – the proof of the Russians' intentions – I saw little hope of convincing the Council. Still, we had to try. Calmer, I forced myself to concentrate. Baranov had come into the chamber.

He was not as ebullient as he had been in the morning. A night spent dozing in the back of Polly Bright's car and a day of interrogation had taken their toll. By now he was tired, even bored. He was not at his best to face another raft of questions, mostly tactful but some dismissive or even hostile.

Once he contradicted himself, suggesting that Sergei was still in Belgium. He was forced to retract what he had said, which annoyed him. He looked at me reproachfully. Hurriedly I fixed my eyes on the green carpet of the Council chamber and the stylized compass rose round which the doughnut-shaped conference table is built.

'I confuse my English,' Baranov said irritably. 'Perhaps Sergei ran away, as the KGB said. Perhaps they took him back to Moscow. I do not know where he is.' He added something in Russian, and the Canadian Ambassador translated: 'For all I know poor Sergei could be in his grave and who would care?'

There was a moment of uncomfortable silence, a movement of bodies, a shuffling of papers, a murmuring of conversation;

somebody coughed. Then the Secretary General reminded us that Baranov had been kind enough not to request an interpreter, and questions began again.

I was on edge. Baranov had made one slip and he could make another, though a mistake about Sergei was almost to be expected. Mr Robinson had insisted that Baranov be given some warning of Sergei's fate and, not to contradict me, had told him that Sergei had run away from the 'safe house' in Brussels where the British had lodged him; perhaps, suggested Mr Robinson, he had decided to return to the Russians. This had upset Baranov and presumably had caused his present confusion. It was a pity, nevertheless.

Now the German Ambassador, who was among the most sceptical of Baranov's inquisitors, was asking him about Marika. He appeared to find it odd that Baranov didn't know how she had escaped from the German Democratic Republic into the Federal Republic, or what had happened to her since.

'She did not tell me,' Baranov said. 'She says it is better I do not know. We meet in Tel Aviv.'

'I put it to you, Monsieur Baranov, that by now she may be back in Moscow, that she may never have intended to go to Israel,' the German Ambassador said suavely. 'My Government has no record of anyone answering her description asking for asylum in the past ten days.'

'And I put it to you, Monsieur, that what you say is – is – ' Baranov produced a spate of Russian.

'Did you examine the watch after she gave it to you, Monsieur Baranov?' the German persisted. 'Are you sure there was anything concealed in it? Maybe Marika wanted you to come and tell us these things about Austria so that NATO should be seen to confront the USSR, and thus threaten the détente. Then, when our fears about Austria are proved groundless, we should be shown up as fools or knaves, and the influence of the Western world would again be weakened. Such things have happened before, you know, Monsieur.'

There was a sudden murmur of interest among the delegates. Here, at last, was an explanation of the known facts, an explanation at least as plausible as the one I was asking them to accept, and much more palatable. I wondered bitterly if it had occurred to Dick or Mr Robinson.

But nobody had much time to consider it. Baranov, who wouldn't have understood the political implications of the German Ambassador's remarks, fully comprehended the personal insult to his Marika. He was on his feet, round the table, shaking his fist under the German's nose and abusing him in a mixture of Russian and English.

'I've been here three years,' the American Ambassador said to me later, after the meeting had been adjourned and we were walking down the corridor together, 'and I've never seen such goings-on in the chamber. It's made my day.'

I had to laugh. 'What do you really think of Heinrich's idea?' I asked. 'I noticed you didn't say much, Seymour.'

He shrugged. 'We can't afford to ignore it, Catherine. Perhaps Marika herself was tricked.'

'We can't afford to embrace it, either,' I said vigorously. 'Not if we want to save Austria.'

'Maybe you're right, at that.' He stopped and turned to me. 'I'll tell you something you may not have heard yet. There're rumours of troop movements in Czechoslovakia and Hungary, not too far from the Austrian border. Of course, they could be just rumours, or Warsaw Pact exercises, or . . .'

'They could be something else.'

He shook his head gently, smiling. 'What I'd give to see that piece of ultrafiche! If there ever was any ultrafiche. Believe me, my dear Catherine, without it your Austrian cause isn't worth a prayer.'

About an hour after this conversation I could have satisfied his curiosity. I knew where the ultrafiche was. I was actually holding it in my hands.

During the afternoon a packet, posted in Brussels on Monday, had arrived at the Residence. It contained the watch and a note. The note said that 'the sick man' – presumably Sergei, though the reference could have been to Mr Robinson – had been so irritated by the strap on his wrist that the watch had been removed, and subsequently forgotten. 'Dick's friend' sent his apologies and best wishes.

I could have wept, but weeping was a waste of time, time that could be better spent deciding what, if anything, could be done with the watch and its precious contents. Now that we had it – too late.

Chapter 17

It was my idea and Dick accepted it. It seemed to be our only chance; we had to take it.

I made myself return to the Forêt de Soignes, this time with Simon – to have asked Hugo would have been unthinkable. We went at the first opportunity, which was not until mid-morning of the following day. Again there had been no alternative. We had to be patient; we couldn't have risked the curiosity of the police patrol at the Residence by going out in the small hours, and it had seemed wiser to go to the office as usual.

Now, at last, we were on our way, speeding through the Forêt in Simon's little MG. The canvas hold-all, which was wedged under my legs, was digging into me, reminding me of its contents; we had come prepared as before. But, because it was daylight, I had decided not to park by La Chapelle de Notre Dame de Bonne Odeur, and instead of the Route de Mont-Saint-Jean we had taken the Chaussée de la Hulpe.

I tried not to think about Sergei Alexandrov.

We left the car a mile or so before Groenendaal and, following a ride, cut across the Forêt. We walked fast and soon reached the Route de Mont-Saint-Jean not far from where we wanted to be. I knew that once we had located the chapel I could find the *sentier*, and then the *piste* which led to the ditch, but I was afraid there might be people about. In the event we saw only a couple of hikers and a party of children on ponies with their riding master. Nobody paid us any attention.

When we were almost at the ditch I let Simon go on alone. It was cowardly of me, I know, but he assured me that he didn't need me, and somehow . . . I leaned against the trunk of a beech in the winter gloom, praying that this would be the end of the nightmare and vowing that I would buy Simon and Polly

Bright the best possible wedding present I could afford. He was back very quickly.

'All right?'

'Yes.' Simon bent over the canvas bag, shutting the zip. 'The body hadn't been disturbed again and I was lucky. I fished up his left arm first thing. It was easy to slide the watch – and the bloody ultrafiche on – on his wrist. But – ' He made a retching sound. 'Sorry!'

'My dear Simon!' I said. 'Come on. Let's get out of here. The next thing's to find a public phone box and ring the police.'

Simon nodded. Obviously he didn't trust himself to speak and we were well on our way to the car before he said: 'I tell *les flics* that I was driving through the Forêt one night this week. I stopped because of my dog. When I called him he didn't come but I could hear him whining. I went to investigate and I found a corpse. I did nothing at the time because I didn't want to get involved, but now my conscience is troubling me. And I tell them where Sergei is.'

'That's it,' I said. 'Then if only someone notices that the watch is Russian made, everything should follow on from there.'

I wasn't as optimistic as I sounded. This was our last ploy and it could so easily fail. Yet Dick had approved it, and Hugo, who came into the office later in the afternoon to arrange for his compassionate leave, was surprisingly encouraging.

'Dick Tindle's a lucky bastard,' he said. 'Things always go right for him in the end. I bet you, my dear Kit, that he'll have you to wife within six months.'

'You'd lose, Hugo.'

'We'll see.' He gave me a lop-sided smile and I thought how ill and haggard he looked. 'Bless you anyway.'

'I've no intention of marrying him – or anyone else.'

But Hugo had gone. He had never believed in lengthy, drawn-out farewells and Daphne's death had hit him hard. He would be glad to forget Brussels for a while.

It was different for me. I was keyed up for the week ahead. And, come Monday, the calm was shattered. Baranov had given a press conference the previous day in Tel Aviv. To judge from the media he had done so with his usual flamboyance but, thank

God, there was no mention of NATO or the British or me. He said that he had abandoned the Bolshoi in Brussels with regret, because he hadn't believed, in spite of the relaxation of the emigration laws, that he would ever be allowed to leave the Soviet Union. He also said that he hoped soon to dance his favourite role, Albrecht, for his friends in the West. Before anything else, however, he intended to marry his beautiful Marika and make a home in Israel.

Marika appeared at his side in all the photographs. She was a short, thick-set girl with a pleasant, intelligent face and a firm jaw-line. Both she and Baranov looked very happy. And, what was most important, her presence vitiated the German Ambassador's argument that she had only been using Baranov to plant the story about Austria at the behest of her KGB masters.

The same evening there was a small discreet item in the news. A body had been found in the Forêt de Soignes not far from La Chapelle de Notre Dame de Bonne Odeur. The face was badly mutilated, but the clothing suggested that the man had come from Eastern Europe. The watch was not mentioned.

I yearned to suggest to my Belgian colleague that this might be the missing Sergei Alexandrov. Even when Tass, the Soviet news agency, admitted that not one, but two members of the Bolshoi had defected in Brussels, I waited for someone other than myself to make the connection. In fact, though I wasn't aware of it, Sergei had been identified almost immediately, the watch had been examined and the Belgian Permrep was in touch with all the right people.

It was Thursday, however, before the North Atlantic Council, in executive session, registered the opinion that the USSR appeared to be planning to violate the neutral status of Austria by using or threatening force. It was unanimously agreed that NATO must take the necessary defensive action to safeguard the Western position in Central Europe. The fat was in the fire with a vengeance. Statements were issued; troops were moved; a major international crisis seemed in the offing.

We had called the Russians' bluff and the diplomats were dancing as Dick Tindle had intended.

*

A month or so later I took some leave. The first night I dined with Dick in his London flat. Sitting across from me in a sparse but not inelegant drawing-room, he raised his glass.

'To you, my dear Catherine, and to all the others who helped to make Operation Overcall a success.'

I drank with him. Appropriately we were drinking champagne; champagne would always remind me of Baranov. 'There's no doubt it is a success? Things still seem pretty tense.'

'But they're improving. Austria's gone off the boil and the Russians can't exploit the situation now – not after all their hurt denials and protestations of innocence. What's more, the Allies have been given a real scare. There's no more talk of withdrawing American forces, or of the Europeans cutting defence budgets. On the contrary! They're all set to give NATO a shot in the arm. And the Russians will heed the warning. Even the hard-liners in the Kremlin will back away from direct confrontation, as we've seen. No, Catherine, not only Austria, but the whole of Western Europe is the safer because of Overcall – at least for the immediate future.'

'That's splendid.'

He looked at me over the rim of his glass. 'Sorry, my dear. I didn't mean to make a speech.'

I laughed. 'Dick – how soon do you think I can resign?'

'You want to resign?'

'Of course. I don't think I'm cut out to be a diplomat, and I want a good, long holiday before – '

'A holiday? In Italy?'

'Italy? Why – Oh no!' I had forgotten that Hugo had just been appointed Ambassador in Rome. I shook my head. 'I'm going to drive down to the South of France. I might even visit Anna de Lisle if she's still in Hyères. Then back to Oxford. I don't much like your "real" world, Dick. I'll be happier in the academic groves of unreality.'

'Will you, Catherine?' He stretched his long legs to the fire. 'I hope not, my dear, I sincerely hope not. But the South of France sounds a good idea.' He smiled. 'Maybe I'll join you for a week or two.'

All Futura Books are available at your bookshop or newsagent, or can be ordered from the following address:
Futura Books, Cash Sales Department,
P.O. Box 11, Falmouth, Cornwall.

Please send cheque or postal order (no currency), and allow 45p for postage and packing for the first book plus 20p for the second book and 14p for each additional book ordered up to a maximum charge of £1.63 in U.K.

Customers in Eire and B.F.P.O. please allow 45p for the first book, 20p for the second book plus 14p per copy for the next 7 books, thereafter 8p per book.

Overseas customers please allow 75p for postage and packing for the first book and 21p per copy for each additional book.